"Something isr
softly.

He pushed Ashlyn into her arms, then drew his gun. "Wait here," he said.

She tried to look past him, but the squirming child made it impossible to see. By the time she had settled the toddler on her hip, Ronin had moved toward the parked vehicle.

Her gaze shifted from him to the Jeep. At first, she didn't see anything wrong, then she realized that both tires she could see from here were flat.

Ronin reached the vehicle and frowned down at the slumped tires. He walked all the way around the vehicle, then stood for several minutes, scanning the area. Finally, he motioned for Courtney to join him.

"What happened to your tires?" she asked when she reached his side.

"They've been slashed," he said. "All four of them, plus the spare."

"Who would do something so awful?"

"I can think of one person."

Trey.

GRIZZLY CREEK STANDOFF

CINDI MYERS

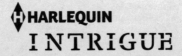

For all my faithful readers.

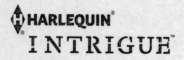

Recycling programs
for this product may
not exist in your area.

ISBN-13: 978-1-335-48952-4

Grizzly Creek Standoff

Harlequin Enterprises ULC
22 Adelaide St. West, 41st Floor
Toronto, Ontario M5H 4E3, Canada
www.Harlequin.com

Printed in U.S.A.

Cindi Myers is the author of more than fifty novels. When she's not plotting new romance story lines, she enjoys skiing, gardening, cooking, crafting and daydreaming. A lover of small-town life, she lives with her husband and two spoiled dogs in the Colorado mountains.

Books by Cindi Myers

Harlequin Intrigue

Eagle Mountain: Search for Suspects

Disappearance at Dakota Ridge
Conspiracy in the Rockies
Missing at Full Moon Mine
Grizzly Creek Standoff

The Ranger Brigade: Rocky Mountain Manhunt

Investigation in Black Canyon
Mountain of Evidence
Mountain Investigation
Presumed Deadly

Eagle Mountain Murder Mystery: Winter Storm Wedding

Ice Cold Killer
Snowbound Suspicion
Cold Conspiracy
Snowblind Justice

Eagle Mountain Murder Mystery

Saved by the Sheriff
Avalanche of Trouble
Deputy Defender
Danger on Dakota Ridge

Visit the Author Profile page at Harlequin.com.

CAST OF CHARACTERS

Courtney Baker—Still grieving for her late husband, Courtney made the mistake of trusting the wrong man, who took advantage of her naivete. She looks weak to others, but when it comes to protecting her daughter, she is able to draw on an inner strength most people don't realize she possesses.

Deputy Ronin Doyle—A newcomer to Eagle Mountain, Ronin moved to the area to pursue his hobby of nature photography, but something besides scenery captures his attention when he meets Courtney. He recognizes the strong woman behind the fragile facade.

Ashlyn Baker—Three-year-old Ashlyn loves Trey because he's the only father figure she's ever known, but Trey takes advantage of that trust.

Detective Jim Fletcher—The Delta police detective is hunting for the leader of a drug ring and believes the man is hiding near Eagle Mountain.

Trey Allerton—Handsome and charming, Trey is an expert at manipulating others, but he doesn't know what to do when the woman who has been his best alibi suddenly turns on him.

Chapter One

Courtney Baker had learned to live with fear. She had grown numb to terror, like an animal paralyzed by an illegal hunter's spotlight. For so long, she had told herself there was nothing she could do. She was too helpless to win in any battle with Trey Allerton. All she could do was endure.

But it turned out, even a trapped animal will fight. Last night when she and Trey argued and he slapped her, the blow had shaken loose something inside her. As she lay beside him that night, after he had told her she was worthless and weak, that she would never survive without him, she had vowed to find a way to leave him.

The determination had stayed with her into the next morning. It was Tuesday, and Trey had errands in town. He must have sensed what Courtney was planning, because he'd insisted on taking her daughter, Ashlyn, with him. Courtney had forced herself to pretend she didn't care, even though inside, her rage burned. This was how Trey controlled her: he used her own daughter as a weapon. "If you try to leave me, I'll hurt Ashlyn," he said. "She'll suffer and it will be all your fault."

Ashlyn loved Trey. Of course she did. She was only three, and Trey was the only father she had ever known. She looked forward to going places with him. He bought her ice cream and new toys and told her how wonderful she was. He had been the same with Courtney when they first met—wooing her with gifts and praise, until she felt treasured and spoiled in a way she never had before.

But once Trey had gotten Courtney to himself, once he had control of her money, he'd turned on her. He sold her SUV, telling her she didn't need it—he could take her everywhere she needed to go. He thought he had trapped her. They lived too far out in the country for her to walk to town, or even to have cell phone service, and he had refused to install a landline at their trailer. And he had Ashlyn as insurance that Courtney wouldn't try to leave.

But lying in bed last night, she had decided to risk leaving. She would walk a quarter mile down the road, to the yurt where a young couple, the Olsens, lived, and ask them for help. As long as she got to the sheriff's office before Trey realized what she had done, deputies could rescue Ashlyn and return her to Courtney. Her sister-in-law, Lauren, and Lauren's fiancé, Shane, a sheriff's deputy, would take them in and protect them until Courtney could find a safe home for the two of them.

The thought of being on her own again frightened her, but now Trey frightened her more.

With trembling hands, she folded some of Ashlyn's clothing, and stuffed them into the single suitcase she had decided to take with her. She tucked in a couple of her daughter's favorite toys and books. She would have to leave everything else behind, at least for now.

She tried to work quickly, to think of everything she would need, but her mind buzzed with a kind of white noise, a static that repeated *What if he finds you? What if he finds you?*

She shut the suitcase and carried it into the living room. It was heavier than she thought it would be, but repacking it would take too much time. She didn't have to carry it that far.

She slung her purse over her shoulder and moved to the back door. Trey would be in town now, far away, but going out the back felt safer. Less exposed.

She stood for a moment in the backyard, though you couldn't call it a yard. It was just an expanse of sagebrush and rock that spread out from the turquoise blue mobile home that had come with the property. A trail through the brush led to a shed where Trey kept tools and other things he had warned her not to touch. She had told him, truthfully, that she had no interest in his belongings, but now she wondered if a smarter person would have been more curious.

She shook her head and picked up the suitcase again. It didn't matter now. She was leaving.

She set off, walking on the shoulder of the road. She was afraid if she tried to cut across country she would get lost. Anyway, it was so quiet out here that she'd be able to hear a car on the gravel road miles before the driver could see her.

She hoped the Olsens were home. No, she wasn't

even going to consider the possibility that they wouldn't be. The young couple were farmers. They had chickens and pigs and goats and a big garden to take care of. They would be at home, working.

The sun beat down, hot and glaring. Her steps dragged a little in the gravel on the side of the road, and her shoulder began to ache. She switched the suitcase to her other hand and kept walking. To take her mind off the pain, she rehearsed what she would say to the Olsens. "Please, I need a ride to the sheriff's office. Trey has kidnapped my little girl. He's threatened to harm her."

It wouldn't be hard to persuade the sheriff that Trey was a bad man. Deputies had already questioned Trey multiple times about crimes in the area. He always had an alibi for why he couldn't have been involved.

Sometimes, she was that alibi. He had told her if she ever tried to retract her statements to the sheriff's deputies, she would be arrested and charged as an accessory. An accessory to what, he never said.

For a long time, that thought had frightened her enough that she'd kept quiet. But that fear, of what might happen, had faded. Maybe she could be charged with a crime, but even jail would be better than staying with Trey, and Ashlyn would be safe with Lauren, who was her godmother as well as her aunt.

Lost in these thoughts, she didn't hear the vehicle approaching until it was almost too late. As the sound of tires on gravel registered, she looked frantically for a place to hide. She spotted a clump of pinion trees, the dark green branches like spiky bottle brushes poking from the gray ground. She dove behind them and crouched, trying to make herself as small as possible. She couldn't see the road from here, so she didn't know if the vehicle was Trey's truck or not. Probably not. It was too soon for him to be back, wasn't it?

She waited a long time after the vehicle had passed, until her breathing had slowed to normal and the only sound was a chickadee calling from a branch above her head. Gravel dug into her knees and sweat trickled down her spine, but still she waited.

Finally, nerves stretched tight, she stood and picked up the suitcase and started walking again.

She could see the entrance to the Olsens' place now—a split rail fence on either side of a gravel drive, with the tall spires of spent yucca blooms clustered in front of the fence.

She clutched the suitcase more tightly and walked faster, her heart pounding.

A hand grabbed her arm, jerking her almost off her feet. She stumbled back, and stared at Trey, who had appeared as if from thin air.

"Where do you think you're going?" he asked. He wore dark sunglasses, hiding his eyes, but there was no mistaking the menace in his voice.

He was a big man—six feet four inches tall, with broad shoulders and powerful muscles. She had thought he was handsome and sexy when they first met. "Wh-what are you doing here?" she stammered. "Where's Ashlyn?"

"Ashlyn is waiting in the truck."

She looked around, but didn't see the truck.

"I saw you when I drove past a while ago," he said.

"Hiding like a frightened rabbit. I parked and walked back." He shook her, her head snapping back and her teeth knocking painfully together. "You're so stupid."

"Wh-what are you going to do?" She regretted the question as soon as she asked it.

He clamped down harder, his fingers digging into the soft flesh of her upper arm. "You'll just have to wait and find out," he said.

DEPUTY RONIN DOYLE slowed as he neared the black Ford pickup parked on the side of County Road 361. At first, he didn't think anyone was in the vehicle, but as he passed, he spotted the car seat, and a hint of blond hair. He drove on, looking for a place to turn around, so he could check things out. Maybe someone had car trouble.

A hundred yards farther on, just around a curve in the road, he saw the couple on the side of the road. A blonde woman with a suitcase, and a big man with his hand on her arm. Ronin hit his brakes, hard enough that his Jeep skidded a little in the gravel. The man jerked his head up at the sound, and let go of the woman.

Ronin put the Jeep in Park, but left the engine running, and got out. "Can I help you with something?" he called.

"Everything's fine," the man answered.

Ronin recognized the man now—Trey Allerton was almost as new to the area as Ronin himself, but had been on the periphery of several recent cases. Ronin hadn't been directly involved in any of those investigations, but he had played a part. One of the things he liked about working for a smaller department, like Rayford County, Colorado was that deputies had a chance to fill a variety of roles. He shifted his gaze to the woman. Her face was sheet-white, her blue eyes huge. She looked terrified. "Ma'am? Is everything okay?" he asked.

She smiled—an expression that transformed her into a real beauty. He blinked, a little stunned at the switch. "Everything's fine," she said. "I'm taking this suitcase to friends down the road and I'm stubborn enough to insist on carrying it myself. Trey was just trying to help."

Trey took the suitcase from the woman. "She didn't want to bother me, even though I told her it's no trouble."

Ronin looked from one to the other. Every instinct told him the story was a lie. There had been real menace in the way Trey held the woman, and real fear in her eyes. But with no one visibly injured and no laws being broken, he couldn't interfere. "Is that your truck back there?" he asked.

"Yes. We need to get back." Trey took the woman's hand. "I don't like to leave Ashlyn by herself for too long."

The woman nodded and followed him back toward the truck. As she passed Ronin, she glanced up, and for half a second their eyes met, her gaze diamond sharp, but undecipherable.

Then she looked away, and walked hand in hand back toward the pickup truck, as if nothing unusual had happened.

Ronin climbed back into his Jeep, but waited a moment before driving on. He was in his personal vehicle, so he didn't have his sheriff's department computer or radio. He wasn't in uniform and he wasn't on duty. And even if, as he suspected, Trey Allerton and his girlfriend had been having an argument on the side of the road, there was no law against that.

He put the Jeep in gear and continued up the road. He had decided to use his day off to drive up to the old Sanford Mine, to photograph the ruins there. An approaching storm had painted the sky with some interesting clouds he thought would look especially dramatic behind the weathered remains of the mine.

A growing interest in nature photography had drawn Ronin to Eagle Mountain from Delta, where he had been an officer with the Delta County Sheriff's Department for seven years. He wanted to be closer to the mountains. So far, the move was paying off. A gallery in Eagle Mountain had agreed to exhibit some of his work, and he'd even sold a few pieces.

He drove to the trailhead leading to the mine, and carried his backpack of camera equipment up the trail. Sun streaked through the clouds, offering the perfect mix of color and shadow for some dramatic images. For the next three hours, he lost himself in his work, taking photo after photo, until the clouds formed a solid gray mass, and rain began to spit.

He had to run the last hundred yards to his Jeep to avoid being completely soaked, but it had been a good day.

But as soon as he was back on the road, he thought of the blonde woman again. Was she really all right?

Trey Allerton had accused the sheriff's department of targeting him. He was a veteran who had relocated to the area to open a camp for disadvantaged kids. He had leased land from a local rancher and spent time soliciting donations from local businesses. Yes, he had sometimes associated with people who had committed various crimes, even murder. But maybe he was just a bad judge of character. Maybe local law enforcement was being lazy, zeroing in on him as a suspect for every crime that came along.

Still, Ronin thought, part of good law enforcement was keeping an eye on questionable people and situations. And it wouldn't hurt to make sure the blonde woman really was all right.

Chapter Two

Trey watched, silent, as Courtney made lunch for Ashlyn, a brooding presence at the door of the trailer's cramped kitchen, his eyes following her as she moved about the room. Rain drummed loudly on the metal sides and roof, fraying Courtney's already abraded nerves and filling the room with watery gray light. The atmosphere of gloom matched her mood, but did nothing to lighten the tension in the air, as if lightning might crackle across the scarred vinyl flooring at any moment.

"I don't want a sandwich," Ashlyn whined. "Trey bought me ice cream."

Another time, she might have scolded Trey for letting the child fill up on sweets, but she didn't have the strength for that now. Trey did what he wanted, and that included spoiling Ashlyn. She wondered if he did it to pit the child against her mother.

"Then come tell me about your trip to town," Courtney said, beckoning Ashlyn to her.

"Later." Trey straightened from where he had been leaning in the doorway. "Go to your room and play now," he said. "Your mom and I need to talk."

If Courtney had given Ashlyn this order, the girl would have argued, or pleaded to be allowed to stay. With Trey, she merely left the kitchen. A few moments later, Courtney heard the door to Ashlyn's room at the other end of the trailer close.

Trey took Courtney's arm and pulled her into their room, on the other side of the kitchen. He shut, then locked the door behind them. The trailer hadn't come with interior locks. Trey had installed this one shortly after they moved in. He had changed all the door locks, too, and he was the only person who had a key.

The suitcase she had packed earlier was on the bed. Trey motioned to it. "Unpack it," he said. "I want to see what you took."

She opened the suitcase and began taking out the contents. "It's just clothes," she said, stacking Ashlyn's T-shirt and pants on one corner of the bed.

"Ashlyn's clothes," he said. "You thought you were going to take her with you."

He moved closer, until he stood beside her, his body pressed to hers, crowding her against the bed. "You were wrong," he said. "If you had gotten away from me, you'd never have seen your daughter again. I'd take her away. You'd have to wonder what happened to her. Maybe I'd kill her. Or maybe I'd sell her to people I know who sell pretty little girls to the highest bidder. Or maybe I'd just give her to someone else to raise. You'd never know. Except you'd know that whatever happened to her was your fault. You chose to abandon your daughter to her fate."

He spoke very softly, his mouth right against her

ear, so that every word buried itself inside her, until she was trembling with rage and fear and grief, as if everything he said had already happened.

She fought against the feelings, and forced herself to look at him, to act as if she wasn't terrified and lost. "I would never abandon her," she said. "Not ever."

"And I won't ever abandon you." He smoothed his hand down her arm, the way a man might soothe a skittish horse or a nervous dog. "I'm always going to look after you," he said. "I promised Mike. You have to let me keep my promise."

His voice was hypnotic, his expression one of such tenderness she trembled with the memories of other times he had been tender. Her mind knew he wasn't really that man, but her body remembered. She had fallen for him so easily after he showed up at her home with stories about her late husband and their great friendship as they served together in Afghanistan. Never mind that in all their conversations and emails, Mike had never mentioned Trey Allerton. Trey knew all about Mike, and about her, and how would he know those things if Mike hadn't told him? Trey had a picture she had sent to Mike—a professional shot of her in a gauzy summer dress, sitting in a field of wildflowers. Trey told her Mike had given him the photo when he was dying and had made him promise to look after Courtney and Ashlyn.

And Courtney had wanted to be looked after. Those two years after Mike died had been the hardest of her life. She had never lived on her own before then, and had never had to look after herself, much less a needy baby, too.

Trey had been so wonderful then—funny, romantic, attentive. Being with him made her feel whole again after all the months of grief and struggle.

Lauren, Mike's sister, had tried to warn her. Lauren hadn't liked Trey from the very first. Courtney had believed Lauren was jealous—Courtney had someone to love who loved her, and Lauren had no one.

"I know this isn't exactly the life you signed up for," Trey said now. He kissed the top of her shoulder and a hot tremor raced through her. "But things are going to get better soon, you'll see. We're going to have the first campers here in just a few weeks and after that I'll have more time to spend with you and Ashlyn."

More time. Was she wrong to think that wasn't a good thing? "Building this camp is a lot harder than I thought it would be," she said.

"Mike would be so proud of you," Trey said. "Of how hard you've worked. And those campers, they're going to remember his name forever. You and Ashlyn will know you've helped to preserve his legacy."

Trey had said that he and Mike had talked of opening a camp for troubled youth—a place where kids from troubled homes or disadvantaged situations could spend time in the outdoors, building their confidence and learning skills that would help them for the rest of their lives. Trey had called the project Baker Ranch, and when he talked about it, Courtney could hear Mike. Her husband had loved children. He and Courtney had talked about having half a dozen. She often wondered what their lives would be like if he hadn't been killed in Afghanistan.

"Things would go faster if we had the money to hire more help," Trey said. "I've been doing everything my-self, and I only have so many hours in a day."

"I thought you'd been raising money," she said. "Lining up donors."

"I've been working on it, but it's a long process. We could use a big infusion of cash now."

He took his hand from her, his expression brighten-ing. "Why don't you make another withdrawal from your trust?" He spoke as if the idea had just occurred to him.

Mike had left Courtney a trust worth several million dollars—money he had inherited when his parents died six years ago. The trust managers distributed a quar-terly allowance that had allowed mother and daugh-ter to live very comfortably before Trey came along. Courtney could also request additional funds for things like education, medical bills, or to buy a home. "You know I can't just ask for money and get it," she said, as if they hadn't already discussed this over and over. "It's not like a regular bank account."

"You're a smart woman," Trey said. "You can think of something."

"Trey, I can't. It looks too suspicious."

"You'll think of something. Get some real money this time, at least 100K." He leaned close again, all signs of the gentle lover vanished, his tone menacing. "Just remember what might happen to Ashlyn if you don't cooperate."

THE CLOUDS HAD cleared and the sun was setting behind the mountains, casting the landscape in an ashy light by the time Ronin pulled his Jeep to a stop in front of the old turquoise mobile home where Trey Allerton and his girlfriend lived. Allerton's pickup was parked in front of the trailer, which sat on concrete blocks amid clumps of sagebrush and gravely earth.

Ronin left the headlights of the Jeep on and crossed through their beams to climb the set of rickety wooden steps to the front door. He knocked on the door and waited.

A full minute passed before a chain rattled and locks turned. The door opened and the blonde from the side of the road looked out at him. "Hello?"

"I'm Ronin Doyle," he said. "I stopped by the side of the road earlier. I wanted to make sure you were okay."

She glanced over her shoulder, then shifted her attention back to him. Light from inside the trailer spilled over her shoulder and illuminated one side of her face, so that she resembled a theater mask of light and dark, comedy and tragedy. "I'm fine," she said.

"Where's Trey?" he asked.

"He went to get something out of his shed—out back." Lines creased her forehead. "Do you know him?"

"I just know who he is."

"Oh. Well, you should leave before he finds out you're here."

"Why? Would he be upset that I stopped by?"

"He doesn't like unexpected visitors." Laughter sounded from a TV that was playing somewhere behind her.

Ronin studied her, as if he could see the truth behind her words if he looked long enough. She was pale and thin and looked vulnerable, but not all strength was determined by a person's size, he knew. Still, something about her—or maybe about the way she had seemed with Trey—set off alarm bells in his head. "What's your name?" he asked.

She hesitated, then said, "Courtney. Courtney Baker."

"It's nice to meet you, Courtney." He took a business card from his wallet and handed it to her. "If you ever need anything," he said. "Anything at all. Call me. I mean it."

She studied the card. "Ronin Doyle. Photography." He'd decided to give her this card in case the one from the sheriff's department frightened her. He had learned that not everyone wanted to confide in law enforcement. "What kind of photographs?" she asked.

"Landscapes, mostly. The Pear Tree Gallery in town has some of my work on display."

"That's wonderful," she said, still staring at the card. "I took some photography classes in school—before I got married."

"You should pick it up again," he said. "There's so many things to photograph in this area."

"Maybe one day." She sounded wistful. She shook her head, then tried to return the card to him, but he refused to take it. "You keep it. Maybe there will be something I can do for you one day."

She started to say something else, but stopped, eyes wide, looking past him.

He looked over his shoulder to see what had caught

her attention. Trey Allerton stood beside Ronin's Jeep. "What do you want?" Trey called.

Ronin took his time turning around and descending the stairs. No need to shout across the yard. He stopped beside the driver's door of the Jeep. "I was on my way home and thought I'd check that everyone was okay," he said.

"How did you know where I live?" Trey asked.

"I saw the truck." Though the truck had only confirmed what Ronin already knew, which was that Trey Allerton had leased this property from the Russell Ranch months ago.

"You're trespassing on private property," Allerton said. "You need to leave."

"As long as you're sure everything is okay."

"Who said it wasn't?" Trey demanded.

"No one." Ronin didn't elaborate. He didn't make a move to leave, either. He wanted to see what Trey would do with the silence.

Trey shifted from foot to foot. "We're fine," he said. "We don't need strangers poking into our business. Understand?"

"Of course." He understood his presence made Allerton uncomfortable, though he couldn't say why. Allerton wasn't nervous, like a man with something to hide. He was more…annoyed that Ronin wasn't intimidated.

"You need to leave," Allerton said again.

"Don't think of me as someone who's butting into your business," Ronin said. "Think of me as someone who's looking out for a neighbor. It's what people do in small towns."

"I told you, everything is fine," Trey said.

"You don't need help setting up your youth camp?" Ronin asked. "I saw some posters about that in town." Allerton supposedly planned to welcome fourteen local boys to a two-week camp next month, a trial run for the bigger program he intended to launch at some unspecified date in the future.

"I've got that covered." Some of the tension left Allerton. "Though we can always use donations."

That was the other thing Ronin had heard about Allerton—he always had his hand out for money. "Maybe next payday." He opened the door of the Jeep. "Nice to meet you, Mr. Allerton."

He took his time turning the Jeep around, aware of Allerton watching him. When he checked the rearview mirror one last time, he saw that Courtney had come out onto the steps and stood, arms hugged across her stomach. She was watching Ronin, too, a still, slight figure in the growing dark, like an image from a Depression-era photo, a woman who was stronger than she looked, with blue eyes that looked toward a future only she could see.

Chapter Three

Courtney Baker was still on Ronin's mind when he reported to the sheriff's department Wednesday morning. The first chance he got, he intended to review the information they had on file about Allerton. But before he could even check the duty roster for the day, Sergeant Gage Walker stopped him. "The sheriff wants to see you in his office," Gage said.

"What about?" Ronin asked.

"You're not in trouble, if that's what you're worried about," Gage said.

Ronin wasn't worried, but Sheriff Travis Walker—the sergeant's older brother—wasn't the chatty sort, and since Ronin had joined the department a month ago, he hadn't exchanged more than a few words with the sheriff. Being singled out now was surprising, to say the least.

The sheriff's door was open, but Ronin stopped and knocked on the doorframe. Travis—tall and lean with dark brown hair and eyes—motioned him inside. "Ronin, come in. And close the door behind you."

Ronin did so, and stood, not quite at attention, in

front of the sheriff's desk. Unlike every other desk in the department, the polished wood surface of this one was visible, only a closed laptop, a single open file folder, and a photograph of a beautiful woman Ronin assumed was Travis's wife, obscuring the polished wood.

"Sit down," Travis said. "How's the job going? Are you settling in?"

Ronin sat. "Yes, sir. The job's going well."

"Good. When you were in Delta, did you know Detective Jim Fletcher, with the police department there?"

"Sure, I know Jim." He had met the detective a few times during training exercises.

"He contacted me about a drug case he's working. He thinks there's a local connection. He'll be here in a few minutes and I thought it would be good if you sat in on the discussion."

Why? was Ronin's first thought, but he didn't bother asking. He'd find out soon enough. Instead, he said, "While we're waiting, let me tell you about an odd encounter I had yesterday with Trey Allerton."

Travis's gaze sharpened, and lines appeared around his mouth. "You were off duty yesterday," he said.

"Yes. I drove up to the Sanford Mine ruins to shoot some photos. I was driving up County Road 361 when I saw a truck parked on the side of the road. A black Ford. I slowed to get a better look and there was a child in a car seat inside. I was looking for a place to go back for another look when I spotted a woman with a suitcase on the side of the road. A blonde who turned out to be Courtney Baker. Trey Allerton was with her, and as I neared them, it looked like they were arguing. He had hold of her arm and it looked to me like she was trying to pull away from him. I stopped and asked if they needed help. Trey told me no. I asked the woman and she said she had been taking the suitcase to their neighbors and the man was insisting on carrying it for her. I'm pretty sure she was lying, even though I couldn't prove it."

"Ms. Baker is Allerton's staunchest defender," Travis said. "Several times when we've questioned her, she's provided his alibi."

"She left with him, but the whole situation didn't sit well with me," Ronin said. "I drove up to the mine and took my pictures, but on the way back I stopped by their trailer. Allerton's truck was parked out front. Courtney answered the door and told me she was okay. She also told me I should leave before Trey found out I was there. I don't know if she was worried about my safety, or about hers if he caught her talking to me. In any case, Trey came up and told me to get lost. I didn't argue, but the whole situation felt off to me."

"Do you have much experience with domestic abuse situations?" Travis asked.

"Some." Given that he had grown up in a home with a volatile father and an abused mother, he could say he'd been dealing with domestic "situations" his whole life.

"You're not the first person to raise concerns about Allerton's relationship with Ms. Baker," Travis said. "But you already know until she makes a complaint or we have evidence of abuse, there's not a lot we can do."

"Yes, sir. I just thought it would be a good idea to have this on record."

Travis nodded. "I agree." He looked up as the office manager, Adelaide Kinkaid, appeared in the doorway.

A sixtysomething widow of a former police officer, Adelaide kept the sheriff's department and everyone associated with it running smoothly with a style that combined the best traits of a den mother and a drill sergeant. "Detective Fletcher is here," she said. "I put him in Interview A because there's no way the three of you are going to fit in here."

Ronin grinned. "Fletcher does take up a lot of space," he said.

Even the interview room felt cramped with Fletcher's six foot seven, three hundred pound bulk in it. His hand engulfed Ronin's when they shook, and the metal folding chair wheezed under his weight. Fletcher wasn't fat, just big and imposing. Ronin had heard that more than one criminal had immediately confessed and pleaded for mercy when confronted with his bulk.

Fletcher opened a file folder and faced Travis and Ronin across the table. "What I've got is a network of drug dealers, all teenagers, who were recruited out of youth groups, sports teams, things like that. The man I'm looking for approaches them, grooms them, then persuades them to sell drugs for him. If any of them are caught, they're juveniles. We don't have that much to hold over them to make them turn on him, and for the most part, he has them all afraid enough of him that they don't talk. But a couple of them have given us some information that indicates the man we're looking for may be somewhere around Eagle Mountain. Which is why I'm here."

"Do you have a name or a description?" Travis asked.

"The only name I have is Smith. Probably an alias." Fletcher paged through the folder. "As for description— he likes to wear costumes. Outlandish ones." He held up a piece of paper. "He befriended some kids in the Delta youth soccer league while dressed as their mascot, the ringtail cat. When he volunteered with a church youth group, he wore denim overalls, a red-and-white-striped shirt, and a blond wig and big-rimmed glasses. All the kids I spoke with said the outfits were purposely out-landish, as if Smith wanted to call attention to them."

"They'd remember what he was wearing, but not so much about him," Ronin said.

"And it worked," Fletcher said. "We have very little to go on. But one boy said he thought Smith told him he had a place near Eagle Mountain. I'm hoping you know something I don't."

"Bart Smith," Travis said. "Though that's probably not his real name. And I have no idea if he's still here, or if he's the man you're looking for, though the cos-tumes sound like him."

Fletcher's expression lightened, and he leaned across the table toward Travis. "Tell me about Bart Smith."

"He came up in connection with a case we handled a few weeks ago," Travis said. "The murder of a young man named Basher Monroe, a rock climber. And the disappearance and attempted murder of another young climber, Cash Whitlow. Smith spoke to the two of them and a third young man, another climber, about needing help on his ranch. He promised money for unspecified extra work. That sounded suspicious to Basher and Cash, and they tried to follow the man, who introduced himself as Bart Smith. They said Smith wore a fake black wig and a wild Hawaiian shirt. After that, Basher was murdered and Cash was shot by a local miner and lost in the wilderness. Later, when Cash had been missing almost two weeks, Cash accepted a ride from a man he believes was Smith. This time, he was disguised as a bald man with an oversize black moustache and mirrored sunglasses."

Fletcher nodded. "That sounds like our guy, including trying to hire young people to work for him. A couple of the kids we've arrested mentioned the same approach. Smith told them he had a way for them to make extra cash. He worked it like a multilevel marketing scheme. He recruited them, and if they recruited others, they could make a cut from each of those transactions, too. Some of these kids were pulling in thousands of dollars a month by the time we caught them."

"We've been looking for Smith, but haven't turned up anything," Travis said. "He didn't kill Basher Monroe, but they had some connection. We found the shirt and wig he wore at the meeting with Monroe and Cash and the third young man in Basher's camper. They all described him as driving a white SUV, but we haven't been able to track that down, either."

"Any uptick in drug activity in your jurisdiction?" Fletcher asked.

Travis shook his head. "Not really. Nothing unusual."

Fletcher's expression grew grim. "This guy has a reputation for being ruthless. The kids say if you cross him, you don't get a second chance. You disappear. We've had a couple of boys in the right age group reported as runaways, but I'm not so sure they really ran away."

"Do you think Smith killed them?" Ronin asked.

"I think your climbers are very lucky they're still alive," Fletcher said.

"I'm asking Deputy Doyle to work with you on this," Travis said.

"I'd really like to stop this guy before he hurts anyone else," Fletcher said.

"The county only has five thousand people," Ronin said. "Someone must know Smith. Probably a lot of them know him."

"There aren't many people here," Travis said. "But there are a lot of places to hide."

"Are you up for this?" Fletcher asked Ronin.

Ronin nodded. He liked challenges, and this one particularly intrigued him. Photography had taught him to look at the landscape in a different way, to see the things other people didn't see. Maybe those skills would help him to find Smith, who was probably hiding in plain sight.

WEDNESDAY AFTERNOON, COURTNEY paused just inside the entrance to the Cake Walk Café. The restaurant was packed with a mixture of local regulars and tourists enjoying the last days of summer vacation. Her sister-in-law, Lauren, rose from a table near the back and waved, and Courtney hurried to her.

"It was so busy I thought I'd better go ahead and grab us a table," Lauren said, and embraced Courtney. She held on a moment when Courtney tried to pull away. "Is everything okay?" she asked. "Where's Ashlyn?"

"Trey took her to Junction with him," Courtney said. "He dropped me off here on their way out of town. You can give me a ride home when we're done, right?" She busied herself unfolding a napkin and spreading it across her lap, avoiding what she knew would be Lauren's expression of disapproval. Lauren always wore that look in any discussion of Trey.

"Why didn't you drive yourself?" Lauren asked.

"We sold my car. We decided we didn't really need two vehicles."

Lauren's eyes flashed, and Courtney steeled herself against what she knew was coming. "It's not safe for you and Ashlyn to be out there with no phone and no car," Lauren said. "How could you think that was smart?"

"It's just temporary." She tried to make her voice light, as if she believed the lie. "And I manage all right. Trey takes me where I need to go, and I come into town often enough to make appointments and stuff in person— just like I dropped by the clinic and made this date with you. I'll get something else soon. Now what should we order? I'm starved." She picked up the menu and pretended to study it.

"Are you sure it's a good idea for Ashlyn to spend

so much time with Trey?" Lauren picked up her menu also but didn't open it.

"Ashlyn adores him." The little girl had begged to go with Trey today, even though Courtney had tried to pry her away with a promise of seeing Aunt Lauren. But Trey had promised a visit to the frozen yogurt shop and Courtney had known she was defeated. "What looks good?" she asked.

But Lauren wouldn't be put off so easily. She leaned across the table and caught and held Courtney's gaze. "You don't think Trey would do anything, well, improper, with Ashlyn, do you?" she asked, keeping her voice low.

"No." Courtney set aside the menu. "I know why you're thinking that, and I thought it, too. I mean, you hear so much in the news." She shook her head. "But I questioned Ashlyn very carefully and it doesn't sound as if he's ever done anything the least bit suspicious."

"But Ashlyn is so young. Would she even know?"

"I asked if he'd ever touched her in a way that made her uncomfortable and she said when they went to Colorado Springs overnight, he combed her hair in the morning and it hurt. She said they slept in separate beds and he made her go in the bathroom and get undressed by herself while he stayed in the other room. He told her she was a big girl and he'd help her with buttons if she needed him to, but he thought she could do it by herself. She was very proud that she did that, though she said he had to tie her shoes for her." She smiled at the memory—of Ashlyn's pride, and of how relieved she had been to hear that nothing untoward had happened.

"So you trust him with her?" Lauren asked.

"I do." She trusted him not to molest her daughter. Whether that was naïve, or a coping mechanism, or the truth, she couldn't decide, and her doubts ate at her. She did believe Trey when he said he would hurt Ashlyn if Courtney ever crossed him. The look in his eyes when he told her those things made her very afraid.

She should say something to Lauren, ask her for help. But she couldn't get the words out. Shame, or fear, or something she couldn't name kept her silent. She was even a failure at asking for help. All she could do was keep pretending everything was all right. "Have you made up your mind?" she asked. "I really am hungry."

She ordered Asian chicken salad while Lauren opted for corn chowder. When the server had left them, Lauren faced Courtney and took a deep breath, preparing to speak.

"How are the wedding preparations coming?" Courtney asked, cutting off whatever Lauren might have been about to say. "Have you decided on a venue? What colors will you have for the decorations and dresses?" Lauren was engaged to Deputy Shane Ellis, whom she had met when she came to Eagle Mountain to search for Courtney after Trey and Courtney relocated here.

"There's a new event center on Dakota Ridge," Lauren said. "They have a gorgeous outdoor chapel that's available for our date, and indoor space for the reception. And I like sage and silver for the colors."

"That sounds beautiful," Courtney said. Her wedding to Lauren's brother, Mike, had also been outdoors, and her colors were blue and white. That seemed like a decade ago, instead of only five years. Had Mike really been gone almost three years?

"Do you think you and Trey will marry?"

The question startled Courtney. "Oh. I don't know. He's never said anything. We haven't talked about it. He hasn't asked."

"Would you say yes if he did ask?"

The thought of marrying Trey, of being tied to him forever, made her stomach hurt. But it was much easier to admit this when she was away from him. When they were alone together he was so good at confusing her feelings. "I know you've never liked Trey," she said.

"And as you've often pointed out, it doesn't matter what I think." Lauren softened the words with a smile. "What matters is what you think. Do you love him enough to spend the rest of your life with him?"

"After Mike, I'm not sure I ever want to marry again," she said. Losing him had been so hard, how could she face that kind of pain again?

"Well, you certainly don't have to rush into anything," Lauren said.

The server delivered their food and Courtney forced herself to eat. She didn't have much appetite lately, but Lauren was sure to comment if she didn't eat it all.

"I've seen the posters around town for the two-week camp Trey is hosting at your place," Lauren said. "Has he had a lot of kids sign up?"

"I'm not sure," Courtney said. "Trey handles those things himself."

"I thought this camp was a project the two of you were working on together," Lauren said.

"It is." Trey had romanced her with talk of the two of them, working side by side to build a legacy that would carry on Mike's name and develop the dream he never had the chance to make come true. She'd given up her comfortable home and her life in the city to come here and make that happen, but things hadn't worked out the way she'd envisioned. "We do work together," she said. "But you know I'm not one for paperwork."

"You don't give yourself enough credit," Lauren said. "You're very smart. You should consider going back to school."

"I'm too busy with Ashlyn," Courtney said, though the idea of going back to college filled her with the kind of longing she hadn't known since she and Mike had agreed to start their family.

"Ashlyn will be in preschool next year. You could start classes online then. What have you always wanted to do?"

"I don't know." She did know, but saying it out loud was too scary, since that dream was so far out of reach.

"Hello, ladies."

The words, spoken by a soft, masculine voice, sent a warm thrill through her. She looked up into the serious gray eyes of Ronin Doyle. "How are you today, Courtney?" he asked.

"Deputy Doyle, I didn't know you two knew each other," Lauren said.

Courtney tore her gaze from his face and took in the khaki uniform, the utility belt and sidearm, and the silver badge pinned beneath the name tag that read Dep. Doyle. "I didn't know you were a deputy," she said.

"I wasn't on duty the day we met." He turned to Lauren. "How are you, Lauren?"

"I'm well, thank you. I saw that you're going to have an exhibit of your photographs at the Pear Tree. Congratulations."

A smile teased the corners of his lips. "Thanks. I've been lucky."

"Talent and hard work have more to do with it than luck," Lauren said. She turned to Courtney. "Did you know Ronin is a wonderful photographer?"

Courtney nodded. "I haven't seen his work yet."

"I'd like for you to see my work sometime. I'd be interested to know what you think," he said, and she felt the weight of his gaze again. He had the most disconcerting way of looking at her, past the surface to something inside of her.

"How is Trey?" Ronin asked.

Courtney stiffened. "He's fine."

"I'd like to stop by and talk to him sometime," Ronin said. "I have a few questions."

"Uh, sure."

He smiled and left them. Lauren leaned forward. "What was that about Trey?" she asked.

Courtney shook her head. The sheriff's department was always asking Trey questions. They seemed to suspect him of all kinds of crimes. Trey was a lot of things—greedy, manipulative, impatient and selfish. He had a temper and he had threatened her and Ashlyn, but would he really follow through on those threats?

How could she have fallen for a man who would do truly bad things?

Trey clearly wasn't the good man she had believed him to be when they first met. She would never admit it, but Lauren was right when she cautioned Courtney not to fall so fast for Trey. *You're still hurting and he's using that to get to you*, Lauren had said. She was right, though Courtney had realized it too late.

She took a deep breath and focused on her salad. Unlike Trey, she wasn't greedy and she could be very patient. After her aborted attempt to leave him, she had decided to outwait Trey. One day he'd get tired of her and she would be able to move on.

"Ronin is a really nice guy," Lauren said. "Good-looking, too, don't you think?"

"I guess." There was no guessing involved. Ronin Doyle had the kind of dark, brooding good looks she had swooned over as a teen, even though she had ended up with two men—first Mike, and now Trey—who had light hair and eyes.

"You'll like his photographs," Lauren said. "He has a talent for capturing the mood of a scene, so that you not only see the stream in the woods, but you get a sense of what it would be like to stand in that scene." She leaned across the table. "So how did you two meet?"

"Oh." She searched for a lie to avoid upsetting her friend. "Trey and I were out walking and he stopped to talk. He wasn't in uniform or anything." And he had stopped by later to check on her. As if he really cared. The idea still made her a little emotional.

"You must have made an impression on him. He made it a point to come over and say hello."

"Mmm." He had made an impression on her, too. But she had his card, slipped into the lining of her bra, where Trey was unlikely to find it. She had started to throw it away, but if she ever did find a way for her and Ashlyn to leave Trey, she thought Ronin would be a good man to have on her side.

Chapter Four

Thursday afternoon, Ronin and Jim Fletcher met with principal Susan Richards at Eagle Mountain High School. "We're concerned about students being targeted by a drug dealer we believe could be working out of this area," Fletcher said after he and Ronin had introduced themselves. "His method in Delta is to approach young people through youth organizations—sports and youth groups."

Ms. Richards, a striking woman with frosted hair in a short, stylish cut and sharply defined features, regarded them with pale blue eyes. "I'm not aware of anything like that," she said. "As you can see, we're a small school, with only about 120 students in four grades. This makes it easier to keep a close eye on everyone. I'm not saying some of our students haven't experimented with drugs, but nothing like you're describing." She turned to Ronin. "Has the sheriff's department found a problem? Is that why you're here?"

"We haven't noticed any uptick in drug activity," Ronin said. "But if the person Detective Fletcher is looking for were to decide to expand into this county, the high school would be a place to start."

"Do you have any adults who volunteer with school sports or clubs?" Fletcher asked. "Particularly any who don't have children attending the school?"

She pressed her lips together, thinking, then shook her head. "The volunteers we have are all parents, and anyone who works with students has to undergo a background check and training. It's our policy."

"It's a good policy," Fletcher said. "Does the name Bart Smith mean anything to you?"

"No. Who is he?"

"It may be one of the aliases used by the man I'm looking for." He passed a business card across her desk. "If you hear of anything or think of anything that might help me, please give me a call."

She studied the card, then tucked it into the center drawer of the desk. "Have you spoken to Art Stevens?" she asked.

"Who is he?" Fletcher asked.

"He runs an after-school program for kids," Ronin said. "Through one of the local churches, I think." He looked to Ms. Richards for confirmation.

"It's a joint project with several churches," she said. "He works with children ages eleven and older. I don't know how many teens he has involved right now, but you should contact him."

"We will. Thanks." Fletcher stood and offered his hand. "It was a pleasure meeting you."

Fletcher didn't say anything until he and Ronin were

in his car. "My high school principal wasn't that good-looking," he said.

"My high school principal was an old man," Ronin said. "Though when I was a teenager I thought everyone over thirty had one foot in the grave."

"I didn't see a wedding ring," Fletcher said. "Is she single?"

"I don't know." Ronin grinned. "Are you interested?"

"I'm going to be staying here for a few days. I might ask her out for coffee." He blew out a breath. "Meanwhile, where can we find Art Stevens?"

"Let me see what I can find out," Ronin said. He took out his phone and dialed the direct number to the sheriff's department.

"Hello, Deputy Doyle," Adelaide answered. "What can I do for you?"

"We need to find Art Stevens," he said.

"He owns a home inspection business," she said. "Works out of a rental upstairs from the newspaper office. If he's not out on a job, you should find him there. I can get you his phone number if you like."

"That would be great. Thank you."

He waited while she looked up the number. "I just texted it to you," she said. "Anything else?"

"Yes. Do you know if Susan Richards at the high school is married?"

"Divorced. Years ago. Her husband is with the symphony in Denver and she has two grown daughters. Why? Are you thinking of asking her out?"

"No. Detective Fletcher needed the information for his files."

"Tell Detective Fletcher if he wants to ask her out he'll need to take her out of town. She doesn't go on dates here in town where everyone will see and talk about her."

"Thanks, Adelaide. Is there anything you don't know?"

"Not much."

Ronin ended the call and turned to Fletcher, whose cheeks were red. "Did you hear all that?" Ronin asked.

"I heard. Does she really know what she's talking about, or is she making it up as she goes along?"

"Adelaide has a reputation as being very reliable."

"Huh. Call Stevens and see if he's in."

Stevens was in, and invited them to stop by his office. Five minutes later, they parked in front of a narrow building sandwiched between a boutique and a liquor store. When they entered, a slender man with a full beard to the middle of his chest and thinning black hair streaked heavily with silver rose from behind the massive oak desk that took up most of one end of the single room. Stacks of books and papers hemmed the man in on three sides. He extended a hand. "Art Stevens. What can I do for you two?"

Ronin introduced himself and Fletcher, who laid out his reason for being there just as he had for Susan Richards. "Ms. Richards told us you're in charge of a youth group in the area," he finished.

"The Explorers," Stevens said. "We're on our fifth year in town. I don't run it by myself, but I'm currently president of the organization. Which means I do everything no one else wants to do."

"I imagine you rely on a lot of volunteers."

"Oh yes. Parents, teachers. People from the local churches. Everyone pitches in to help."

"Do you have any new volunteers?" Fletcher asked. "Particularly someone who doesn't have a child in your program?"

Stevens smoothed his beard. "No one new. We pretty much rely on the old faithful. And certainly I would notice anyone who took an undo interest in the children." He sighed. "Unfortunately, you have to be so careful these days. We don't allow any kind of inappropriate behavior and we have a policy that none of our volunteers ever works alone with the children. We require background checks, eight hours of training, and there are always at least two and usually more, adults present."

"Do you know anyone named Smith?" Fletcher asked. "Bart Smith?"

"No. I haven't heard that name."

Fletcher handed Stevens a card and told him to call if he thought of anything.

"I hope you catch the man you're looking for," Stevens said. "One of the things we try to do in Explorers is stress the importance of staying away from drugs and alcohol. There are always going to be some kids who experiment with forbidden fruit, as it were, but we try to provide alternative activities with a positive focus. We've helped a lot of young people over the years."

"How did you get involved in the program?" Fletcher asked. "Do you have children?"

"I don't. But I come from a troubled background. Things could have turned out bad for me, but a teacher took me under his wing and got me involved in a youth organization very similar to the Explorers. I wanted to help other kids the way I'd been helped."

They left the office and headed back toward the sheriff's department. "What do you know about Stevens?" Fletcher asked.

"He has a good reputation," Ronin said. "I think he's received awards for the work he's done with local kids."

"Reputation can be a cover for some pretty bad stuff," Fletcher said. "I've known award-winning coaches and revered pastors who turned out to be abusing kids."

"I haven't been in town that long," Ronin said. "I can ask around, see if there are any rumors or hints of past trouble."

"Do that. It just seems odd to me that a man with no children of his own would be so dedicated to them."

"He's grateful for the help he received as a teen."

Fletcher glanced at him. "Do you believe that?"

"I decided to go into law enforcement because of a youth boxing program run by local cops in the town where I grew up," Ronin said.

"No kidding." Fletcher straightened. "Well, we always hope the things we do make a difference. I guess sometimes they do."

The bad things people did made a difference, too, Ronin thought. It was one more reason to try to stop them before they inflicted a hurt that couldn't be overcome.

Chapter Five

"Have you contacted your lawyers about getting that 100K I need?"

Courtney was scrambling eggs for breakfast Friday morning when Trey asked this question. She glanced at him, trying to read his mood, but he looked calm, as if he'd asked if she'd remembered to pick up coffee creamer at the store.

She turned her attention back to the eggs. "I haven't been anywhere to call them." Cell phones didn't work here, and Trey had refused to pay to have a landline installed. One more way to keep her dependent on him.

"You should have called Wednesday, when you were in town."

"It wouldn't matter," she said. "I can only withdraw the money to pay for education, medical expenses or to buy a house. Last time I got money to make a lease payment on this land. I can't use that excuse again."

"Tell them it's time to build a new house," he said. "Or to remodel. It doesn't matter. It's your money. They can't keep it from you."

"You know a trust doesn't work that way."

"So now you're saying I'm stupid?" He rose, his chair scraping back from the table, the sound sending a shiver up her spine. "I know how a trust works. If you made any effort at all, you could get the money we need."

"What happened to the money from selling my car?" she asked. She hadn't wanted to sell the little SUV—her best means of escape from here. But Trey had badgered her all night, alternating between cruel and consoling, until she had given in and signed over the title. Now she had to rely on him to take her shopping or to the doctor or anywhere else she wanted to go. She prayed there wasn't an emergency when he wasn't around.

"I spent it on the next lease payment. And we have bills, you know. Electricity and television and insurance and groceries. Not to mention construction costs. We're supposed to have fourteen campers here in just a few weeks and we need to have tents and food and restrooms and all kinds of other things for them."

He was getting worked up, pacing back and forth, gesturing with his hands. Any second now, he might turn that anger on her. "You're doing a great job," she said.

"Everything depends on me." He stopped beside her. "Withholding money is your way of making sure I'll fail. Is that it?" He grabbed her arm and shook.

She forced herself not to react. She didn't pull away or cry out or do anything but keep silent and wait.

He released her and went back to pacing. She switched off the burner beneath the cast-iron skillet.

"Today, you're going to write the lawyers a letter," he said. "Tell them whatever you need to tell them to get that money. If you've put it down in writing, they can't argue with you."

And there was no arguing with Trey.

"I'll try," she said. "That's all I can do."

"You'll do it right after breakfast. Then I have someone coming to see the place."

"Who?"

"None of your business. But change into something pretty and fix yourself up. Don't embarrass me in front of this guy."

Trey used to tell her how pretty she was, and how much he liked to show her off. She knew she didn't look as nice as she once had. She'd lost weight, and she had dark circles under her eyes from not sleeping—not to mention bruises on her arms where Trey was always grabbing her.

She moved to the door of the kitchen and looked into the living room. Ashlyn sat on the floor in front of the television, a brightly colored cartoon playing in the background. But Ashlyn wasn't watching the screen. She was arranging a quartet of dolls in front of her, talking softly to them. "We're going to go for a long ride now," she said. "But if you're good, I'll buy you an ice cream sundae."

"It's time for breakfast," Courtney said. "Come on before it gets cold."

Ashlyn left the dolls and followed Courtney into the kitchen.

"Trey, are we going somewhere today?" Ashlyn asked as she took her seat at the table.

"Not today," Trey said. "I'm going to work here, then I have some things to do in town by myself."

"I want to go with you to town," Ashlyn said.

"Not today," Trey said.

"But I want to go!" Ashlyn's voice rose in a whine.

"Ashlyn, no," Courtney scolded.

"If you don't shut up, I'll never take you with me again," Trey said.

Courtney glared at him. "You don't need to talk to her that way," she said.

"It worked, didn't it?" He took a bite of egg, his expression smug.

Ashlyn was quiet now, her cheeks red. She stared at her plate, not eating.

"Eat your eggs before they get cold," Courtney coaxed.

"Eat them or I'll throw them out," Trey said.

"That's no way to talk to a child," Courtney objected.

"You spoil her. Ashlyn, eat."

Ashlyn ate, but Courtney's appetite was gone. She pushed her food around until Trey finished his meal. Then he stood. "You can write that letter after you clean up the kitchen," he said. "I'll be out in the shed."

"Why is Trey mad at us?" Ashlyn asked after the door closed behind him.

"He's just in a bad mood this morning." Courtney scooped Ashlyn out of her chair. "Why don't the two of us play dress up?" she asked. "You can help me fix my hair, and we'll find something really pretty for you to wear."

"Yes!" Ashlyn clapped her hands. This was one of her favorite games to play. She and her mother had spent many a long afternoon in the trailer trying on clothes and makeup, and experimenting with different hairstyles. Ashlyn ought to be playing with children her own age, Courtney knew. But this was the best she could do right now.

In the bedroom Courtney shared with Trey, she slid open the closet doors and surveyed the dresses and blouses hanging there. "Wear this one, Mommy." Ashlyn fingered the skirt of a sundress printed with pink and gold roses.

"All right." Courtney took the dress from the hanger and laid it on the bed. She glanced out the window and saw Trey walking toward the portable shed he'd erected several hundred yards from the house. He'd said he needed it to store tools and some of his belongings, but she had yet to see inside of it. He kept it locked and had told her more than once she was not to "go snooping" in his things.

Which of course only made her more curious about what he was hiding. Maybe some of the money he'd talked her and lots of other people into giving him was in there. He was always soliciting for donations, and he was so charming she knew he must have been successful. Sure, there were bills to pay, but those couldn't have eaten up all that money, could they?

"Mama, I want to wear this!" It was another sundress, short and strapless and bright orange and yellow tie-dyed swirls.

"All right, honey. But you'll have to let me help you with it." Folded and belted, the dress would look cute on her little girl.

For the next hour, Courtney forgot about Trey and lawyers and money and everything else as she combed and braided Ashlyn's hair, and curled her own locks into big, loose waves. They put on their pretty dresses and Courtney spent time on her makeup, contouring and shading, lining her eyes and layering on four coats of mascara. She dusted Ashlyn's face with a little glittery highlighter and added the faintest hint of pale pink lip gloss, then let her apply one spritz of perfume. "Mommy, we look so pretty!" Ashlyn said as they admired their reflections in the dresser mirror. "You look like a princess."

"A princess who has to clean the kitchen now," Courtney said. And think of what to write to her lawyer.

She was rinsing the last of the breakfast dishes in the sink when the back door opened and Trey came in, followed by a man with a long, bushy beard and thinning black hair, the man's pale scalp showing through his comb-over.

"Art, this is Courtney," Trey said by way of introduction.

"Art Stevens." The man held out his hand and Courtney wiped hers on a dish towel, then shook.

"It's good to meet you," she said. "Would you like some coffee? I can make more."

"No, thank you. I never have more than one cup in the morning."

"Have a seat and you can give me those names," Trey said. He pulled out a chair for Art, then sat across from him.

Courtney started drying the dishes in the drainer by the sink, curious to know what business this man had with Trey. He seemed less, well, menacing, than some of the others Trey had brought here.

"We've got several teens in the Explorer's Club who would really benefit from a getaway at your camp," Art said once he was seated. "Of course, most of them would probably love an excuse to spend two weeks in the mountains, hiking and riding horses and being with friends. Who wouldn't?"

"I'm interested in helping those who need it the most," Trey said. "Kids from troubled homes, maybe with a family history of addiction, or financial difficulties. One of our focuses is on giving young people the tools to break that cycle of poverty and abuse."

"I understand, and I definitely have some candidates in mind."

Courtney wiped dishes and put them away, most of her attention attuned to Trey as he described the programs he had in mind for the children who attended his camp—horseback riding, art therapy, nature study, games and exercise—it all sounded wonderful. But how was he going to offer all that when he had no horses or games or therapists, or even tents for the kids to sleep in? He said he was going to buy all those things, but could he really do all of that in three weeks?

"Right now, I can only take boys," Trey said, in response to Art's mention of a girl he thought would benefit from the camp experience. "I don't yet have separate facilities for girls. Or female staff."

You don't have any *facilities*, Courtney thought.

"Yes, it's a good idea to keep things separate," Art said. "Best to focus on boys first. Now these three young men…"

Courtney put away the last clean dish and moved into the living room, where Ashlyn was playing with her dolls again. She took a notebook from a drawer in the end table and a pen.

"Can I have some paper to draw?" Ashlyn asked.

"Sure." Courtney handed over a pen and paper and sat on the sofa, Ashlyn beside her.

"What are you going to draw?" Ashlyn asked.

"I'm writing a letter," Courtney said. Whatever she wrote needed to sound like a serious plea for funds. Trey would read this before he mailed it and she needed to satisfy him. But could she also find a way to alert the attorney that something was wrong, without alarming Trey?

She supposed the request itself would raise suspicions. Before Trey had persuaded her to contact the trust several months earlier, she had never requested anything outside of her usual quarterly allowance. She had had to work hard to persuade the attorney in charge of the funds to give her the money. She had even resorted to lying, but only because she believed it was necessary. That was when she still believed in Trey's dream of building a camp to help children.

But no matter how beautiful that dream was, she didn't think she could be a part of it much longer. Her desire to help other children couldn't take priority over her duty to help the one child who mattered most to her. She had to leave Trey and the dream behind in order to protect Ashlyn.

But she needed to be clever. And cautious. She picked up her pen and began to write.

RONIN GLANCED AT the book on the passenger seat of his Jeep. He'd pulled it off his bookshelf when he'd come home after his shift today. *Essentials of Photography.* It still had the sticker from the campus bookstore where he'd purchased it in his undergraduate days. At the time, his impulse had seemed like a good one, but now he wondered if he was being foolish. Maybe he was stirring up trouble where he shouldn't.

He turned onto the county road, gravel popping beneath the undercarriage of the Jeep as he left the pavement. Another hour or so and he might be able to catch the alpenglow on Dakota Ridge. He could say that was why he'd come out here. Not that he'd made a special trip to give a woman he hardly knew one of his old textbooks.

A woman who was living with another man, his conscience reminded him.

It was just a book. He could be nice to someone without having other intentions.

He slowed as he neared the driveway leading up to the mobile home. No black pickup out front. If Trey's truck had been there, Ronin would have driven past and spent the rest of the evening shooting. It would probably be time better spent.

But he turned into the drive and drove up to the trailer. He picked up the book and got out before he could change his mind, and headed for the door.

He heard music as he mounted the steps—something bright and upbeat, a female singer he didn't recognize. He knocked hard to be heard over the music, and a moment later, Courtney answered the door.

She looked different today. She was wearing makeup, and a pretty dress, her hair in ringlets framing her face. He caught a whiff of floral perfume, too. "Am I interrupting something?" he asked, trying to look past her without being too obvious.

She smiled, and he felt the impact of her happiness in the middle of his chest. "Ashlyn and I were having a little party, dancing around." She held the door open wider. "Do you want to come in?"

She was so different from the tense, almost silent woman he had encountered before that he kept staring, making sure this was really the same person.

"What brings you here, Deputy Doyle?" she asked, with an emphasis on his rank.

"A couple of things." He held out the book. "I came across this and thought you might like it."

She took the book and studied the cover. "You want to give this to me?"

He felt stupid. Why had he thought she'd want his old textbook? But he was all the way in this now. Better to keep plowing forward. "You said you were interested in photography."

She looked up from the book and when her eyes met his, another jolt shook him. She was blinking back tears. "That was very thoughtful of you. Thank you." She looked around for somewhere to put the book, and ended up slipping it into the drawer of a little table by the sofa.

"Maybe you'd like to go with me some time to take photos," he said.

She looked amused. "Are you asking me on a date?"

His face heated. "No. I just thought, if you want to renew your interest in photography…"

"There are so many photographers in this area," she said. "It's amazing, really."

"Everyone brings something different to it," he said. "The photos you would take wouldn't be the same as the photos I'd take because you bring your own perspective to each shot."

"Maybe I will try my hand at it one day," she said. "For now I'm pretty busy looking after Ashlyn."

The little girl appeared in the doorway, holding up her long dress with both hands so she wouldn't trip on the hem. She stared up at Ronin and released her hold on the skirt and began to gnaw on one fist.

Courtney scooped the girl into her arms. "This is my daughter, Ashlyn. Ashlyn, this is Deputy Ronin Doyle."

"Hello, Ashlyn." The child was beautiful, with a cloud of golden curls spilling beneath a circlet of braids, and big blue eyes just like her mother's.

"Why else did you stop by?" Courtney asked. "You said the book was one reason. Was there another?"

Because I wanted to see you again, even though that's probably a really foolish thing to do, he thought. "I wanted to see if you were all right," he said instead.

"Why wouldn't I be all right?" The lightness had left her expression, and her voice held a chill.

"When I saw you the other day, with Trey, I had the sense something wasn't right."

"Just a lovers' quarrel."

Did he imagine the emphasis on *lover*? Was this her way of telling him to back off?

"I guess I misread the situation." He took a step back. "Keep the book. I hope you find it useful."

He had enough dignity not to run from the trailer, though that's what he felt like doing. Best to get out of here and focus on photography until the light was gone. With his emotions in such turmoil, it would be interesting to see what kind of photos he took.

"Ronin," Courtney said, but he was already in his Jeep and turning around. She covered her mouth with her hand and turned back inside, Ashlyn already squirming to be let down. "I want to watch *Blue's Clues*," Ashlyn said, and picked up the television remote.

While Ashlyn sang along with the theme song for the show, Courtney sank onto the sofa and hugged a pillow to her stomach.

What had she done? Ronin had given her the perfect opportunity to tell him that yes, she was in trouble. Could he wait ten minutes while she packed her and Ashlyn's things and then he could take them away from Trey Allerton and his threats and promises?

So why had she lied? Worse, why had she spouted that nonsense about a lovers' quarrel?

The answer was a cold hand gripping her stomach. She had lied because she was afraid. Not of what Trey might do to her or to Ashlyn if they left him, but of what he would do to this nice lawman if Ronin helped them.

She had spent a lot of time and energy telling herself that Trey wasn't really dangerous, but in her gut she remembered the power in his hands when he hit her and the coldness in his voice when he belittled her. She remembered people he had quarreled with who weren't alive anymore. Sure, other people had confessed to killing those people. But how much of a role had Trey played in those murders? Maybe none.

Or maybe a lot. So when Deputy Ronin Doyle had offered his help, that part of herself locked deep inside that recognized what Trey was really like and what he could do had recoiled in horror and rushed to push Ronin away.

Now she felt stupid and sick.

But she felt a little braver, too. She'd done a good thing, acting to protect someone else. Maybe all the lies she had told for Trey, and all the people she had hurt, hadn't completely destroyed the good in her. Maybe she was still strong enough to look after herself.

She didn't need Ronin Doyle. All she needed was to find a way to make Trey more afraid of her than she was of him. Proof that he had stolen or killed or committed some other crime would do it. When she had that kind of information she could take it to the sheriff or use it as a bargaining chip with Trey to buy her freedom.

The idea made her feel giddy. She had a plan now. All she needed to do was carry it out.

Chapter Six

"We've made another arrest of one of Bart Smith's recruits," Detective Fletcher said when he and Ronin met for lunch the following Monday. They ate at a picnic table outside a new food truck near the town park. Ronin had spent the morning on foot patrol in the area between the park and the high school. He had helped a teacher who had locked her keys in her car, issued a warning for a dog running loose in the park and directed a tourist to the town library, but had seen no suspicious activity. "Who did you arrest?" he asked.

Fletcher plucked a French fry from beside his sliced beef sandwich and chewed it before answering. "A sixteen-year-old who was recruited by Smith. He fit the pattern we've established—basically a good kid with no criminal record who is in a troubled family situation. He met Smith playing hoops at a local park." He took a drink of iced tea and continued. "Smith befriended the boy—no pressure at first, but when the kid opened up about his situation—parents just divorced, a disabled younger sibling who gets all the attention, money problems due to the divorce and the sibling's medical issues—Smith suggested the kid come to work for him as a way to fund his independence. At first it was just running errands, delivering packages and messages, but it evolved to dealing drugs to other students. As far as we can tell, the kid wasn't using himself, and he was raking in the cash and feeling good about the whole deal. Then we arrested him and he was scared half to death. We offered to protect him from Smith and he told us everything he knows. Unfortunately, it's not a lot."

"Do you still think Smith is from Eagle Mountain?" Ronin asked.

Fletcher nodded, chewing, then said, "He told our witness that he had a ranch here, which lines up to remarks he made to another boy who was working for him."

"Did you get a description?"

Fletcher frowned. "We did, but it's another of Smith's disguises, or rather, a costume. This kid says the first time they met at the park, he thought Smith had been in an accident, or burned. Half his face was really scarred. It was so awful, he avoided looking directly at Smith, which I guess was the idea. He said Smith usually wore a beanie pulled down, covering his hair, and dark glasses, even at night. He had yellowed teeth and talked with a lisp, so we think the teeth may have been fake."

Ronin took a bite of coleslaw and considered this. "You'd think a man with a scarred face would be easier to find," he said after a moment.

"Except the scar was probably fake and Smith ditched it whenever he was away from his recruits."

"Did you get anything else useful from this boy?" Ronin asked.

"He saw one of the missing boys—Dallas Keen—with Smith once. That confirms our suspicion that Keen was working for Smith, too. Keen has been missing almost two weeks now. Our witness may have been one of the last people to see him before he went missing. He said he was sitting in the passenger seat of the white SUV Smith was driving—a Toyota, he thinks, with mud on the license plate. He noticed Keen because he had a black eye and a busted lip, as if he'd been in a fight. He asked Smith if Keen was okay and Smith said he was fine, not to worry about it. Our witness says Keen never looked at him, or even raised his head."

"And you don't have any clue what happened to Keen?" Ronin asked.

Fletcher ate another fry. "He'd been gone three days before anyone reported him missing. Another kid who was pretty much left to fend for himself. His parents are together, but they're both alcoholics. The dad works in the oilfield and is gone a lot and the mom has just checked out. His grandmother called in the report, but she lives in Denver, so she'd just learned the boy hadn't been home in three days."

Ronin nodded, thinking of the weeks in high school when he had drifted from one friend's house to another, his parents not even bothering to check where he was.

They focused on their food for the next several minutes. "I did some checking up on Art Stevens," Ronin said when he'd eaten the last of his chopped beef sandwich. "He doesn't have a criminal record. Not even a traffic violation. Distinguished military service, then a solid career. Not even a vague rumor of anything suspicious. The only complaint I heard from anyone was from a former volunteer at the Explorer's Club who said he was a stickler for following rules. Apparently, this woman was asked not to come back when she didn't follow the proper guidelines for chaperoning an outing."

"He doesn't sound like someone who'd stand for one of his people recruiting in his organization," Fletcher said. "But we know Smith is smart, and cautious. He might find a way around Stevens's rules. Or he might look elsewhere."

"Troubled kids can crave attention," Ronin said. "The right kind of relationship, with a caring teacher or coach, can make a positive difference, but they're just as vulnerable to the wrong influence."

"Smith knows how to take advantage of that." Fletcher wiped his hands on a paper napkin, then pushed the wrappings from his meal aside. "It's a frustrating case, but we're going to catch him. He's going to make a mistake. He's too cocky, with all these wild disguises, and I feel like he thinks he's safe here in the mountains."

"People who feel that way usually find out they're wrong," Ronin said. "For one thing, anything out of the ordinary stands out in a small population. For another, the local cops aren't stupid."

"Why did you leave Delta to come here?" Fletcher asked.

"I'm a photographer. I was spending all my spare

time out here taking photographs. When I heard there was an opening here I decided I should work and live closer to where I wanted to be anyway."

"Huh." Fletcher picked up his cup of iced tea. "Are you any good?"

"I'm getting better," Ronin said. "I have my work in a gallery here and I've sold a few pieces."

"I guess if you get tired of the law enforcement gig, you'll have something to fall back on." Fletcher shifted on the hard bench. "Speaking of local attractions, I've got a date tonight with Susan Richards."

Ronin grinned. "I guess the attraction was mutual."

"Your office manager was right—I had to promise to take her into Junction. After I'm done here I'm going to clean out my car and run it through the car wash."

"I'm sure she'll be impressed."

Fletcher scowled, but there was no heat behind the look. "Aren't you single?" he asked. "Did you leave someone back in Delta?"

"Yes. And no."

"You dating anyone here?"

He thought of Courtney Baker, whom he was not dating, and whom he couldn't date. "I've only been here a month," he said.

"You should take advantage of the fact that you're a new man in town. I imagine the dating pool is pretty small in a place like this."

"I'm in no hurry to work my way through it," Ronin said. He didn't necessarily like being alone, but relationships were complicated and it was nice to take a break from that.

Fletcher pushed himself up from the bench. "I'll let you get back to work."

Ronin tossed his trash in the bin and set off across the park again, headed toward the sheriff's department. He hadn't gone far when his radio buzzed. "Deputy Doyle, the sheriff wants you to meet him by the quarry on Brentmeyer Drive," the dispatcher's crisp voice said.

"I'm about five minutes from my vehicle," Ronin said. "Then I'll head that way."

"I'll let him know to expect you."

Ronin thought about the summons on his way to his sheriff's department SUV. Whatever the reason for the summons, it hadn't sounded urgent, but the lack of detail made him suspect it was something Travis didn't want the general public who listened in on the police band to know about.

Brentmeyer Drive turned out to be a narrow dirt lane off a county road at the far northern end of the county, in a barren landscape of rock outcroppings and sagebrush. Ronin spotted the crime scene investigation van alongside several other vehicles, including two Rayford County Sheriff's Department SUVs.

The sheriff walked out to meet Ronin as he pulled his SUV in line with the others and parked. "A retired guy whose hobby is collecting fossils was out here exploring and smelled something dead," Travis said. "He took a closer look and found a body. I think it might be one of the missing kids Fletcher is looking for. There's a Delta High School hoodie, jeans and basketball shoes."

"I was just having lunch with Fletcher," Ronin said.

"We'll get him out here later, but I wanted you to have a look first, since you're working this with him here in the county."

"Should I bring my camera?" Ronin asked. He often photographed crime scenes for the department. He wasn't the designated photographer, but he had the equipment and skills and put them to use when needed.

"That's all right. Someone's already on that."

Ronin followed Travis along a path defined by yellow flags, He smelled the remains before he saw them. A stocky older man in a Tyvek jumpsuit crouched over the body. He looked up at their approach. "Decomposition is too advanced to tell me how long he's been out here," he said. "Maybe I'll know more when I have him back at my lab."

The sheriff introduced the county coroner, Butch Collins, then said, "We've got some mud on the rocks over there." He pointed to their left, and an area cordoned off with yellow and black crime scene tape. "Some faint tire impressions. It's been ten days since the last recorded rainfall here."

"That fits with what I'm seeing here," Collins said. "But I'm not making any definite declarations. At this point, I can't even tell you how he died. The most I can give you is that the victim was male and fairly young."

Ronin studied the terrain around them. "Could he have been climbing on these rocks and fallen?" he asked.

"If he did that, how did he get here?" Travis asked. "We're at least three miles from the nearest house, and that's a ranch where no one under the age of sixty lives. I'll talk to them, but if someone was missing from there, they would have reported it."

"He could have been with friends, and they got scared and left," Ronin said.

"He could have," Travis said. "We'll look into that." He turned away from the remains, and joined Ronin in studying the barren landscape. "I'm not ruling out anything at this point, but I have a feeling we're looking at another murder."

AFTER MONTHS OF talking and planning and fundraising, work had finally begun on their new kids camp—Baker Youth Ranch. Courtney had choked up when she first saw the sign Trey had erected near the entrance to their property. "I can't believe it's really happening," she had said, and clutched Trey's hand.

"We're going to do a lot of good here," he said. "We'll help a lot of kids." He gazed up at the sign. "When I think of all the times Mike and I talked about this day. He'd be so proud of this."

Now the sounds of hammers and power tools filled the air as a pair of men Trey had hired built a pavilion and outdoor kitchen where the campers would eat meals and constructed wooden platforms for the big tents that would serve as sleeping quarters until more permanent cabins could be built. Trey had printed a brochure with a map of the camp, showing hiking trails, a meeting area with benches and a fire pit, and shower and restroom facilities, all of which he said would be completed very soon.

Courtney wondered where the money for all of this

was coming from. Trey had mailed the letter she had written to her lawyers, requesting money from her trust, but even if they released funds from her trust it could take weeks before she had the cash in hand. Was Trey gambling on having the money before the bills for all this construction came due?

Or maybe he had been saving all the donations he'd received as a result of his fundraising efforts. Some of the tension she'd been holding inside eased at this thought. The doubts that had sometimes crept into her mind—that Trey might be keeping the money for himself—made her feel a little guilty now. Yes, Trey had a temper and was a little self-centered, but he had devoted himself to building this camp to help children. She needed to remember that.

"I've got business in town," he told her Monday after lunch. Tomorrow would be a week since she tried to leave him and she was no closer to coming up with a plan for her and Ashlyn to safely get away.

"Can I go with you?" Ashlyn asked.

He smiled at her. "Not today, sweetie. You stay here with your mom." Trey looked up at Courtney. "Stay in the house and don't bother the workmen."

"Why would you think I'd bother the workmen?" she asked, annoyed at his assumption.

"Just stay away from them. They're busy. And I've told them not to talk to you."

The meaning behind his words sank in, and she felt weighted down by it. *Don't think of asking one of the workers for help*, Trey meant. *I've already warned them about you.* What had he told them? she wondered. Did he say she was delusional or unbalanced? A liar who wasn't to be believed? Or maybe he had portrayed himself as the kind of jealous man who would fire anyone who spoke to his girlfriend.

"I've got plenty to do here at the house," she said.

This wasn't true. She was bored to tears most days. She could only clean so much, and the trailer was so shabby and poorly furnished she had no desire to try to improve things. She remembered her beautiful home in Denver, with its comfortable furniture and carefully chosen decor. Trey had convinced her to sell it with his stories of the mountain ranch they would share, with a beautiful log-and-stone cabin in a forest of trees. She had cried the first time he showed her this old metal trailer surrounded by sagebrush and cactus. He had promised this was only temporary, but she still missed her old things.

After he left, she played with Ashlyn for a while, Trey's admonition to stay inside grating like sand in her shoe. She started packing away the art supplies she and Ashlyn had been using. "Let's go for a walk," she said. She wasn't going to say anything to the workers, but she had every right to see the work they had completed so far.

Ashlyn was happy to get out, and raced ahead of Courtney, stooping to pick up rocks or to look at a column of ants marching across the ground. They followed a well-worn path from the trailer to the shed where Trey stored his tools. The camp structures were going up just beyond, at a high point on the property which offered a nice view, as well as a stretch of fairly level ground on which to build.

As they neared the storage shed, Courtney realized the large padlock that usually fastened the door was hanging loose, unfastened. Her steps faltered and her heart rate increased. Trey always kept that shed locked. He said it was to deter thieves, but she had always believed it was partly to keep her away from his things. The idea hadn't bothered her much—she had assumed he kept souvenirs from his army days, perhaps guns and ammunition in addition to the pistol he kept locked in a case in their bedroom drawer, or perhaps a stack of porn magazines. She didn't care about any of those things.

But seeing that lock unfastened piqued her curiosity. She glanced around. Trey was still gone, and the workmen couldn't see her from their position up the hill.

Before nerves got the better of her, she hurried toward the shed. Ashlyn hung back. "Trey told me never to go in there," the little girl said. "He said there was a bad thing in there that would get me."

How dare he make up lies to frighten her daughter. "There's nothing bad in the shed," she said. She picked up Ashlyn and settled the child on her hip. "How about we go in together? I promise to protect you."

Ashly chewed the side of her fist, but nodded.

Courtney slipped the hasp of the lock from the staple and pulled the door open. The wood had warped slightly and she had to tug hard, but it came open. She peered into the dark interior, and inhaled the scents of dust and oil.

After staring into the dark for a moment, she made out the shape of a flashlight on a shelf beside the door. She picked it up and switched it on, then played the beam across the shed's contents.

A row of tools hung on one wall—a shovel, a hoe, a rake and a set of garden shears. A coiled water hose was piled in one corner, and a metal shelf at the back held various bottles, boxes and cans. A large footlocker sat in front of the shelf, a heavy brass padlock secured at its front. The army souvenirs, she decided. Maybe guns.

She stepped inside, hip cocked to balance Ashlyn, who joined her mother in studying the various items filling the small space. Several unlabeled cardboard boxes were stacked double along the wall opposite the garden tools, a battered khaki backpack on top of the boxes.

She moved closer to examine the backpack. She couldn't remember seeing it before. A leather patch on the outside pocket had a set of tooled letters—a monogram. MKC, the K larger than the other two letters.

The letters didn't correspond to Trey's name, so who did the pack belong to?

She propped the flashlight beside the pack and used her free hand to tease open the top zipper. Then she picked up the light and shone it on the interior of the pack.

She blinked as the light bounced back to hit her in the eye. It took a moment for her to register what she was seeing: the pack was half-filled with little gold bars, each about the size of a candy bar. At first, she thought they might be candy—fancy chocolates wrapped in gold foil. But when she reached in to pick one up, the weight startled her. The bar was heavy and solid. She tried to pick up the whole pack with one hand and couldn't it. Closer inspection showed where the straps were separating from the pack and the seams strained, as if from the weight of the load.

"Pretty," Ashlyn said. She leaned closer to look at the gold bar in Courtney's hand.

Courtney stared at the bar. There was writing on it—numbers and letters she didn't try to decipher. She was certain this was real gold. Would anything else be as heavy or shiny?

She tried to count the bars in the pack, but without taking them out she couldn't be certain how many there were. But they must be worth a lot of money.

Was this how Trey was paying for the new construction at the camp? Had some very generous donor given him the gold, or had he used the donations he had received to purchase the gold? Some people preferred precious metal to cash in the bank, though Trey had never talked about anything like that.

A gust of wind banged the door of the shed against the side and she jumped, and almost dropped the bar in her hand, which she guessed weighed about as much as a canned soft drink, and was about two inches by three inches wide and around half an inch thick. Instead of returning the bar to the bag, she slipped it into her pocket. Maybe later she would ask Trey about the gold.

Or maybe she would keep this one bar a secret. A source of emergency funds in case she needed them.

Chapter Seven

"We have a positive ID on the young man whose body was found near the quarry." Travis started the Tuesday morning meeting with this news. "Dallas Michael Keen, sixteen, from Delta."

"Detective Fletcher's missing person," Ronin said.

"Yes. I've notified Detective Fletcher and I've shared a copy of Dr. Collins's report." The sheriff consulted his tablet again. "No definite time of death owing to decomposition, though Butch guesses at least a week. The tire impressions were most likely made after the last rain we had, eleven days ago."

"Any idea what kind of tires?" Deputy Wes Landry asked.

"There's not enough tread pattern for an ID," Travis said.

"Do we have a cause of death?" Gage asked.

"No broken bones, so that rules out a fatal fall," Travis said. "No bullets found in or near the body and no sign of gunshot trauma to the bone or the soft tissue remaining, so Butch is ruling out gunshot. Toxicology came up negative. The report notes there's a great deal of blood on the front of the victim's shirt, which could be indicative of a knife wound, such as a slashed throat, but 'decomposition is such that a definite determination cannot be made.'" Travis read this last statement directly from the report.

"What's his final assessment?" Gage asked.

"Suspicious death, cause undetermined," Travis said. He set aside the tablet. "Let's interview everyone who lives in that area. And we'll put out a public appeal for any information about suspicious activity at the quarry around the time of that last rainstorm."

"I want to talk to Art Stevens again," Ronin said. "Find out if he knew Dallas Keen. I know Keen was from Delta, but Art may have seen him around, or know of a reason he might have been here."

"Talk to Fletcher first," Travis said. "He may have already interviewed Art."

"Still no leads on Bart Smith," Landry said. "Since he likes costumes so much, I wondered if he might be an actor or someone involved in film or theater, but I'm not finding anything."

Ronin contacted Fletcher as soon as the meeting was over. "I'm on my way to talk to Stevens right now," the detective said. "You're welcome to come with me. I'll swing by and pick you up."

"Stevens is on a job today," Fletcher said when he picked up Ronin at the sheriff's department. "He said we could meet him there."

Stevens was doing an inspection on a home in Idlewilde Estates, a new development of high-end homes not far, as the crow flies, from the ranch where

Courtney Baker lived. Art Stevens met them in front of the garage. "I'm doing an inspection for the new buyer," Stevens said. "The homeowners aren't here, so I can take a few minutes to talk to you."

"Do you know a teenager named Dallas Keen?" Fletcher asked.

"No. That name doesn't ring a bell. Is he a local kid?"

"He's from Delta."

"I know all the local teens," Stevens said. "But Delta is a little far away for the kids to do much socializing."

"Maybe you've seen him around." Fletcher showed Stevens a picture of Keen.

Stevens studied the picture then shook his head. "I don't think I've ever seen him. Why are you looking for him? Is he in some kind of trouble?"

"He was killed and his body was dumped at an abandoned quarry near here," Fletcher said.

Color drained from Stevens's face. "That's horrible. Who killed him? Do you know?"

"We don't know, but we intend to find out," Fletcher said.

Stevens turned to Ronin. "When did this happen?" he asked.

"A week to ten days ago," Ronin said. "The body was just discovered yesterday."

"I hope you find whoever did it soon. I hate to think of any kid being hurt."

"Have you thought any more about the questions we asked you the other day?" Fletcher asked. "Can you think of anyone who's taken an unusual interest in the kids you work with? Anyone who made you uneasy?"

"No one," Stevens said. "Like I told you, our program vets the volunteers very carefully. For the most part, we've been working with the same people for years. Mostly parents and a few teachers."

"Have you had anyone apply to the group that you've turned down?" Ronin asked.

Stevens rubbed his chin. "There was a guy three years ago. Turned out he had been charged in a domestic violence case three years before. He said he'd turned over a new leaf, but we still had to turn him down. We couldn't risk it."

"How about inquiries about volunteering, maybe from someone who didn't follow through?" Fletcher asked.

"None," Stevens said. "I'm sorry. I don't think I'm being much help to you." He checked his phone. "And I really had better get back to work and finish up this job."

They left him. "What do you think?" Fletcher asked when he and Ronin were alone in his car.

"I think he's telling the truth." Ronin glanced over at the house, a two-story timber-frame structure of stucco and stone, with a metal roof designed to naturally rust. "Maybe we're not coming at this from the right angle," he said.

"What do you mean?" Fletcher started the vehicle then pulled away from the curb.

"Maybe Smith isn't expanding into this area at all. Maybe he doesn't want to foul his own nest."

"Maybe our witness heard wrong, or maybe Smith was going to expand here and changed his mind. But I had to check things out, and leaving Keen's body here in your county isn't too smart if Smith wants to avoid pressure from law enforcement near his home base."

"We don't know for certain that Smith killed Keen," Ronin said.

"No. But the last time anyone saw Keen alive, he was with Smith, and the other boys Smith recruited were afraid of him. He made them believe he'd kill them if they crossed him. I think Keen is proof he wasn't bluffing."

"Then maybe we need to look beyond Art Stevens and his youth group," Ronin said.

"I've spoken to people at the school and local sports leagues," Fletcher said. "So far they haven't come up with anything."

"How about a youth camp for troubled kids?" Ronin asked.

"Those posters around town," Fletcher said. "I've seen them. I even called the number on the poster and got a voice mailbox. I left a message, but no one returned my call."

"The man who's setting it up doesn't like law enforcement," Ronin said.

"I take it he's had run-ins with the law before?" Fletcher asked.

"He doesn't have a record," Ronin said. "He's never even been charged with a crime. But he has been a known associate of at least two murderers in this county, and he was a neighbor to a third."

"That sounds like more than coincidence," Fletcher said. "Who is this man, and where can we find him?"

"His name is Trey Allerton. He lives on some ranchland out County Road 361."

"Tell me how to get there," Fletcher said. "I definitely want to talk to him."

TREY TOOK ASHLYN with him when he left the trailer Tuesday. Did he suspect Courtney was up to something, or was this just his usual practice to remind her how much was at stake if she made a wrong move? But finding the gold had reenergized her. With money, it would be easier to pay for safety from Trey. She could travel far away, and hire attorneys, even a private bodyguard. But one bar wouldn't be enough. She needed more. She was debating going back out to the shed to explore further when a plume of dust announced the approach of a vehicle. A black sedan rolled slowly down the road, toward the entrance to their property. It stopped by the new sign, then swung into the drive. Courtney stood back from the window and watched as the car parked, then Ronin Doyle and another man got out. Ronin was wearing a Rayford Country Sheriff's Department uniform, while the other man wore dark slacks and a blue polo shirt.

She thought about not answering when Ronin knocked on the door. Not because of Ronin—he had always been kind to her. But she didn't know the man with him, an older man whose expression told her he didn't think much of the trailer or its surroundings.

When Ronin knocked a second time, she opened the door. "Hello?" The greeting was more of a question, the words *Why are you here?* and *Is something wrong?* behind the two syllables.

"Hello, Courtney. This is Detective Fletcher. May we come in?"

Could she say no to that request from a law enforcement officer? "Trey isn't here," she said. "I'm not comfortable inviting a stranger in when I'm alone." She glanced at Fletcher.

"We just have a few questions." Fletcher took a wallet from his hip pocket and opened it to show his badge and identification. "All aboveboard. Deputy Doyle can vouch for me."

"We can talk outside, if you're more comfortable with that," Ronin said.

She shook her head and held the door open wider. "I guess you can come in." It wasn't exactly a warm welcome, but Fletcher had aroused her curiosity. So many officers had come to the house to talk to Trey over the past few months. It really did seem like they suspected him of every crime that happened in this little county, and she couldn't figure out why. She knew a less pleasant side of Trey, but with everyone else he was so charming. But Detective Fletcher's ID said he was with the Delta Police Department. What did they want with her or Trey?

She led them to the sofa and sat. Ronin sat at the other end of the couch, but Fletcher remained standing. "Where is Trey?" Fletcher asked. He looked around, as if he half expected Trey to rise up from behind the bookcase.

"He went to a meeting. I don't know with whom," she said.

"I see you've got some construction going on up the hill," Ronin said.

"Yes. They're starting work on some buildings for the camp. It's nice to see things starting to take shape, after so many months of planning."

"I've seen the posters around town," Fletcher said. "You're going to have kids camping out here in a few weeks?"

"Three weeks," she said. "Just a dozen or so to start. By next summer we'll have facilities for many more."

"How are you finding your campers?" Fletcher asked.

"There are the posters you mentioned," she said. "And I think Trey has contacted schools and church groups to let them know about the program."

"Can just any kid sign up?" Fletcher asked. "Or are there certain requirements?"

"Requirements? What do you mean?"

"Oh, you know." Fletcher waved one hand. "Some camps are specifically for athletes or math nerds or kids with diabetes—things like that."

"Oh. Well, I know we're only taking boys at first, until we have more facilities. Then we can welcome girls, too. And we really want to help more disadvantaged children, those whose families have less income, or who are from single-parent families. Maybe kids who are struggling in school. Trey—we—feel a calling to especially help those children."

Fletcher looked thoughtful. "So, a school counselor might recommend a boy for the program—someone who's struggling in school or dealing with a family crisis?"

"Yes. We want to give those kids extra attention and a chance to get away from their everyday problems."

"So you have counselors who can help these kids?" Fletcher asked.

"We will." She tried to sound confident. She had always assumed they would hire professional counselors, but Trey hadn't mentioned it in a long time. "Of course we'll have professionals to help," she added.

"Who has Trey talked to about recommending boys for the camp?" Fletcher asked.

"I don't know. You'll have to ask Trey. Why do you want to know?"

"Do you know the names of any of the boys who have signed up for the first camping session?" Fletcher asked, ignoring her question.

"I think that's private information," she said. "Why would you need to know that?"

"In Delta, where Detective Fletcher works, there's been some trouble." Ronin spoke for the first time in a while. "Someone has been recruiting teenage boys to sell drugs. We want to prevent the same thing from happening here."

"We would certainly never let anything like that happen here." Relief swept over her. Of all the things they might have accused Trey of, this was the most farfetched. "Trey takes a very dim view of drug abuse," she said. "He's said so many times. If anything, he wants to have programs at the camp that emphasize staying away from drugs."

"We're not accusing Trey of anything," Ronin said. "But it's possible that someone he hires to work for him might be connected to the people in Delta who have been recruiting teens."

"Does the name Bart Smith mean anything to you?" Fletcher asked.

The name sounded familiar. She looked at Ronin. "Wasn't someone with the sheriff's department looking for someone named Smith after that missing climber was found last month?"

"The climber, Cash Whitlow, said a man named Bart Smith had threatened him," Ronin said.

Courtney looked at Fletcher again. "That's the only time I've heard the name," she said.

"Where did you live before you moved here?" Fletcher asked.

She really wanted to tell him that was none of his business, either, but she didn't have the energy to argue over something so trivial. "I lived in Denver."

"What about Trey? Did he live in Denver, too?" Fletcher asked.

"Trey is from Colorado Springs. He was stationed there while he was in the army. After he served in Afghanistan he returned there, until we decided to move here."

Fletcher took out a business card and laid it on the coffee table. "Call me if you notice anyone acting suspicious with your campers," he said. "Things like separating one boy from the others or too much one-on-one time between a counselor or other staff member and one of the boys."

"All right."

Fletcher looked at Ronin. "I'm done here."

"You go on out," Ronin said. "I'll be along in a minute." He didn't move from the sofa, and waited until Fletcher had left before he spoke again. "We didn't mean to upset you," he said.

"You didn't upset me." She smoothed her hands down her thighs. "I know the sheriff's department doesn't like Trey, but he would never hurt a child. He's devoted himself to building this camp to help children."

"He's made some poor choices of associates in the past," Ronin said.

"Well…yes." When they had first moved to Eagle Mountain, Trey had taken on a business partner, Tom Chico, who had murdered his girlfriend, and maybe other people, too. And then had hired a handyman from a local ranch, Von King, and he had killed the rancher he worked for. "I think Trey is too idealistic and trusting," she said. "And maybe he isn't the best judge of character." She had never liked Tom or Von, but Trey had been deaf to her objections.

"How have you been?" he asked, his gaze so intense she had to look away.

"I'm fine."

"Do you get lonely, here by yourself when Trey is gone?"

"I'm not alone. Ashlyn is usually with me."

"Is Ashlyn here now?"

She looked away from his searching gaze. "No. She's with Trey."

She sensed his disapproval. Or maybe a better word

was *concern*. Did he think she was a bad mother for allowing Trey to spend so much time alone with Ashlyn? But she didn't have any choice. She wasn't strong enough physically or smart enough mentally to fight Trey. She wanted to tell Ronin that she was doing her best. But that would mean telling him the truth, and that felt too risky. She spotted the photography textbook he had given her, and picked it up from the coffee table. "I've been reading this," she said. "Thank you again."

"I hope you're able to pick up some things to use in your own photography," he said.

"I don't have a camera," she said. "Just my phone."

"Phones these days can take very good pictures," he said. "Sometimes the art is in the composition, not the equipment."

"I don't know what I'd take pictures of."

"Your daughter. The landscape. This is your world, and photographs are a way to invite others in."

The idea intrigued her—and made her a little nervous. She wasn't sure she wanted to invite others into her world. "I'd like to see your photographs one day," she said.

"I'm having an exhibition of my work at the Pear Tree Gallery on Saturday," he said. "Just a little reception beforehand, then the pieces I've chosen will remain on display for the rest of the month. You should come."

"Oh no. I mean, I don't have a way to get there."

"I could give you a ride."

She could only imagine what Trey would say to that.

"That's very kind of you, but I'd better not." Her eyes met his, silently pleading for understanding. Whatever he saw in her gaze made him stand abruptly. "I won't keep you any longer," he said, and strode to the door and out before she could even think of a reply.

She would have liked to attend his opening—to put on a pretty dress and do her hair, and spend a few hours sipping wine and eating hors d'oeuvres and talking about art with a handsome man who looked at her as if she had things to say that were worth hearing.

Even Mike hadn't looked at her that way. He had loved her. Even adored her. But the look she most remembered from him was the expression people assumed when gazing upon a much-loved pet. Here was someone precious, to be protected and cared for.

She had been caring for herself and Ashlyn for a long time now. She didn't need a caretaker nearly as much as she needed someone to listen to her, and to treat her as a person with a brain and good ideas.

These days, she craved respect more than romance. Did that mean she was smarter, or only more jaded?

"DOES TREY ALLERTON know you've got a thing for his wife?"

The knowing look Fletcher gave Ronin when he returned to the car, even more than the question, annoyed Ronin. "She's not his wife, and I don't know what you're talking about."

"You're not much of a poker player, Doyle," Fletcher said. "If it's any consolation, she's attracted to you, too."

"You questioned her for five minutes. You don't know anything."

Fletcher laughed. "I know I got a rise out of you." He focused on his driving and changed the subject. "This youth camp is worth keeping an eye on. It's the kind of setting where Smith could cut a vulnerable kid from the pack and groom him to be one of his recruits. It fits the pattern he's used before."

"How do you know Smith is really in Rayford County?" Ronin asked, forcing his focus back to the job at hand. He didn't have to like Fletcher, but he did have to work with him. "Maybe he's still in Delta."

Fletcher shook his head. "Our sources say not. We made things too hot for him there. The two kids who've told us the most both say he planned to move the whole operation to his ranch near Eagle Mountain. Allerton has a ranch, so he's moved up my suspect list."

"It's just a bunch of vacant land," Ronin said. "It isn't a ranch, just a leased part of a ranch."

"It's close enough for me," Fletcher said. "Maybe we should try to get someone in there undercover, once the camp opens."

"You'd have to talk to the sheriff about that," Ronin said.

"Better to bring in someone from our department," Fletcher said. "We've got a couple of rookies who could pass for teenagers with the right clothes. I'll talk to Travis about it. Meantime, you keep a close eye on the girlfriend."

"Why?" Ronin asked.

Fletcher laughed again, a sound that was starting to

really annoy Ronin. "Because I think she knows more than she's saying," Fletcher said. "And because it gives you an excuse to keep seeing her. If Allerton ends up out of the picture, you'll be right there."

Ronin started to protest that he wasn't interested in Courtney that way, but Fletcher would see through the lie. If Courtney Baker wasn't already involved with someone else, Ronin would have asked her out. If Trey Allerton did turn out to be connected to this case, that would only complicate things for him and Courtney.

Not that he minded complications. Sometimes a bit of a struggle made reaching a goal more rewarding. But Courtney wasn't a prize for him to win. She was a woman who deserved better than she had now. Whether or not he was the person to give that to her—he guessed that was up to her to decide. But he liked the idea of putting himself on her list of options.

Chapter Eight

After Ronin and the detective left, Courtney opened the drawer in the coffee table and pulled out the book Ronin had given her. *Essentials of Photography.* She stroked her hand over the cover, with its illustration of a camera imposed over an array of snapshots—a landscape, a portrait, an action shot and a still life. Then she opened the cover.

Ronin Doyle—his name inscribed in thin, slanting letters. Why had he given this to her? They had only talked, briefly, a few times. Was he simply the kind of person who liked to pass on items he no longer had use for to someone who might appreciate them?

Or had he recognized the longing in her for something outside the increasingly small world she felt trapped in? Was he throwing her a lifeline—a reminder that she could be more? Do more? Have more?

Tears burned her eyes and she closed the book and tried to remember everything she could about him. He had kind eyes. Not soft or even gentle, but there was understanding in them, as if he, too, had experienced hard things.

Or maybe she was imagining all of that. She had done that before, with Trey and even with her husband, Mike. She had thought of them as what she wanted them to be. Maybe they had done the same with her. Maybe that was how romances worked—romance gave you the ability to gloss over faults and only see the ideal.

That was romance—but what about love? Love required a clearer vision, the ability to see the whole person, good and bad, and accept it all. Just as they accepted you.

That was the kind of relationship she wanted. Real and raw and stronger because it could accept the bad with the good. She knew there were people out there like that and she wanted to be one of them.

Courtney was preparing dinner when Trey returned home. She heard him and Ashlyn come into the house and tried to gauge what mood he might be in by the sound of his movements. She looked up expectantly as he approached the kitchen, hoping the Trey who greeted her would be the easygoing charmer she had fallen for, and not the sullen taskmaster she had grown to fear. "Where's Ashlyn?" she asked, surprised the little girl wasn't with him. Ashlyn usually came running to Courtney as soon as she returned home.

"I sent her to her room," he said.

"Why? Is something wrong?" She turned off the burner on the stove and started toward the door into the rest of the house. Trey put out a hand to stop her. "Leave her. You and I need to talk."

The words sent a jolt of fear through her, but she

tried to hide it. She returned to the stove. "How was your trip to town?" she asked, smiling at him.

He didn't return the smile, or come to kiss her. Instead, he walked past her to the refrigerator and took out a bottle of water. "Who was here while I was gone?" he asked.

The question startled her. She focused on the vegetables she'd been chopping and tried to gather her thoughts. "How did you know someone was here?" she asked.

"I saw the tire tracks in the dust of the driveway. Then there's this." He held up a business card. "'Detective Jim Fletcher, Delta Police Department,'" he read. "Detective Fletcher is a long way from home. What did he want?"

"He wanted to talk to you." She spread the vegetables—red potatoes, carrots, bell pepper and onions—on a cookie sheet.

"What about?"

"He wanted to know about the camp and the kids who would be coming here. He wanted to know if we'd hired any counselors to help."

"What business is that of his?" Trey twisted the top off the bottle of water and tossed it on the counter. It landed amid the carrot and onion peels beside her.

"He said...he said someone has been recruiting teenagers to sell drugs. I think he thought they might try to hire on at a place like this."

Trey drank half the bottle, then said, "What did you tell him?"

"I told him he needed to talk to you."

"What else did he say?"

She drizzled olive oil over the vegetables. "He asked if we knew a Bart Smith."

"Smith was who that deputy asked about after they found that missing climber," Trey said.

"I think so." She sprinkled salt on the vegetables. "I told him we didn't know anyone named Smith."

"Was Fletcher by himself?"

"He had a local deputy with him."

"Who?"

"Deputy Doyle."

"The photographer." Trey smirked. "Your admirer."

His tone of voice, and the expression in his eyes, sent a chill through her. "I don't know what you're talking about."

"No? He gave you that book you've been reading. His name is in it." He finished the water and set the empty bottle on the counter, then leaned close to her. She could feel the heat of his body, and smell his sweat. "Since when are you interested in photography?"

"I took some classes before I married Mike. I'd like to know more."

"Do me a favor and don't encourage the deputy to hang out here."

"I'm not encouraging him." She opened the oven and slid in the tray of vegetables.

Trey gripped her arm. "You didn't tell them anything, did you?"

"No, of course not." She tried to pull away, but he held her firm, his fingers digging in. "What would I tell them?"

"Nothing. It's like we agreed—what I do is none of their business."

He released her and took a step back. Her arm ached, and the pain made her angry. "What do you do?" she demanded. "You're gone all the time. You never tell me what you're up to. I thought we'd be partners in building this camp. But you're the one making all the decisions."

She had feared her question would anger him. Instead, he looked amused. "You're busy with Ashlyn and taking care of the house."

"That doesn't take all my time. I could help you with the camp. This is supposed to be our project."

He nodded. "Sure. Of course you can help. What do you want to do?"

"I could help with hiring staff. We're going to need counselors, and someone to cook for the kids when they're here."

"They're old enough to cook for themselves," he said. "It's a valuable life skill."

"What about the counselors? If our focus is on helping troubled teens, we'll need professional help."

"That will come later. I told you before—this first group of campers is just to get our name out there and generate some positive publicity and more donations. These will be local kids. No big-city problems."

As if only children from the city had problems. "You can't do this all by yourself," she said.

"I don't have to. I've got you." He slung his arm around her and pulled her close, crushing her against him. When she tried to pull away, he asked, "Hey, what's wrong?"

She thought of the gold in the shed. Where had it come from? "Are you keeping secrets from me?" she asked.

He took his arm from around her and moved away. "It's none of your business if I am," he said, then left the room.

She held on to the edge of the counter, shaking with anger, and with fear. How could she have ever believed she loved a man who was so cold?

She had spent the last few months lying to herself—pretending Trey was the man she needed him to be, someone she could trust to look after her and Ashlyn. When they first met, she had believed he was so much like Mike, a strong man who would love her and take care of her and her daughter. She thought that was what she needed. It was what she needed when she married Mike, but she was a different person now. She didn't want to be taken care of, not if that meant giving up making her own decisions and choosing her own path. Independence—having to be on her own—had frightened her for so long.

Now all she wanted was the chance to make her own choices, and her own mistakes. If only she could get away from the man who had been her biggest mistake yet.

RONIN SPENT THE rest of Tuesday afternoon reviewing the department's file on Trey Allerton. He told himself he was looking for a possible link to the case he was working with Jim Fletcher, but a voice in his head nagged that he really wanted to know everything he could about the man who had attracted Courtney Baker.

There was a lot to sift through, from the department's initial encounters with Trey after Courtney's sister-in-law, Lauren Baker, reported her missing, through the murder of a local young woman, Talia Larrivee. Trey's business partner at the time, an ex-con named Tom Chico, had turned out to be the murderer. Trey swore he had nothing to do with the crime, and Courtney Baker had provided him with a solid alibi.

Flash forward a few weeks and the murder of local rancher, Sam Russell. Trey had been a suspect because he leased sixty acres from Russell, and had finagled a deal that both extended the lease indefinitely and reduced his rent to a dollar a year in the event of Sam's death. But again, Courtney had provided Allerton's alibi. The real murderer turned out to be ranch hand Von King, who had also worked part-time for Trey.

More recently, the sheriff's department had questioned Allerton about the disappearance of climber Cash Whitlow and the murder of Whitlow's friend Basher Monroe. The two young men had encountered a shady character who introduced himself as Bart Smith and had tracked Smith to the area near Allerton's home. But they had never been able to establish a link between Smith and Allerton, and once again, Courtney Baker had provided an alibi for Allerton for the time of Monroe's murder. The real killer had been Allerton's neighbor, a reclusive miner named Martin

Kramer. Kramer, awaiting trial for the killing, claimed he had shot Monroe in self-defense.

So Trey Allerton had been on the periphery of every major crime the sheriff's department had dealt with that year, but the only thing he appeared to be guilty of was associating with the wrong people.

Courtney hadn't struck Ronin as a liar, but he knew that just as people might kill to protect the ones they loved, they would commit lesser sins as well—like lying. The thought depressed him and he forced himself to focus once more on work.

Adelaide appeared in his doorway. The office had an intercom system, but she often preferred to deliver her messages in person. Today the white-haired office manager wore earrings in the shape of black cats with garnet eyes, and red-framed bifocals. "There's someone here who wants to speak to a deputy," she said.

"Who is it?" he asked.

"Martin Kramer's daughter."

"I didn't know Martin Kramer had a daughter." Nothing in the file he'd just read had mentioned any relatives.

"Neither did anyone else," Adelaide said. "Can you talk to her?"

"Of course."

Elaine Kramer Schaeffer was a tall, physically imposing woman with long auburn hair and worried brown eyes. She offered a firm handshake after Adelaide made the introductions, then sat on the edge of the chair opposite Ronin's desk, her purse in her lap. "I want to know what your department is doing about locating the gold that was stolen from my father," she said.

Ronin remembered a passing mention in the file to gold her father had claimed Basher Monroe had been trying to steal. "I wasn't aware the gold was actually missing," he said, speaking carefully. The consensus seemed to be that Martin Kramer was an eccentric who made up the gold story. The mountains around Eagle Mountain were pocked with defunct gold mines that had either never produced a profit, or had been played out a hundred years before.

"It's definitely missing," she said. "My father regularly transported ore he took from the mine to a smelter in Pueblo, where it was processed and turned into gold bars. He kept the bars in a strongbox inside the mine. I visited there earlier this week and the strongbox was missing." She leaned forward. "My father needs that money for his defense," she said. "Even if you think he's a murderer, you have a responsibility to investigate this theft."

"Yes, ma'am. This is the first credible report we've had of a theft." He opened a file on his computer and began making notes. "What was the value of the stolen gold?"

"Just under forty thousand, though of course, the price of gold fluctuates."

Ronin stilled. "That's a lot to keep at home," he said.

"It wasn't at home, it was in the mine, in a locked strongbox that was sunk into solid rock."

He noted this, then asked, "Does your father know who took the gold?"

"He said people were always nosing around the mine."

"But what people? Any names?"

She frowned. "He mentioned neighbors. There was a young couple who brought him vegetables from their garden, and baked goods. He liked them. I don't think he believes they stole from him. There was a man who lived down the street. Dad said he was always too interested in the mine."

"Do you know his name?"

"Troy something."

"Trey?"

"Maybe that's right."

"Anyone else?"

The lines of her frown deepened. "The night that young man was shot, Dad believed he was trying to steal from him. Him and his friend. Maybe they succeeded."

"We haven't found any gold in possession of either of them," Ronin said.

"Then I don't know who took the gold. You need to find them. It's not as if gold bars are that common."

"I promise you, we'll look into this," Ronin said. He collected a little more information, including how to get in touch with her, then she left.

Ronin typed up his notes, aware that once more, he would need to question Trey Allerton about the missing gold.

He was reviewing what he had written when Jim Fletcher strode into the room. "You look hard at work," Fletcher said, sinking into the chair Ms. Schaeffer had recently vacated.

Ronin saved his file, then gave Fletcher his full attention. "What have you been up to?" he asked.

"I've been doing some checking up on Trey Allerton."

"Oh?" He couldn't get away from the topic of Trey Allerton today.

"He's not the man I'm looking for," Fletcher said. "Though if he hires any employees at that camp of his, I'll want to look at them very closely."

"What made you rule out Trey?" Ronin asked.

"The man doesn't have so much as a traffic ticket," Fletcher said, a note of disdain coloring his words, as if he found it difficult to believe anyone could be so innocent. "He's got an excellent military record, and everyone I spoke to sings his praises."

"That wasn't the impression I got," Ronin said, the details of Allerton's file fresh in his mind. "When he was stationed in Colorado Springs, he was brought in for questioning a couple of times, in relation to various crimes."

"Right. But nothing ever came of those." The chair creaked under Fletcher's bulk as he leaned forward. "The guy does have a habit of hanging out with the wrong people, but all that tells me is that he's a terrible judge of character."

"Maybe you're right," Ronin said. "But I don't think it would hurt to keep an eye on him."

Fletcher rapped his knuckles on the desk. "You're just saying that because Allerton's girlfriend has gotten under your skin. No—don't try to deny it. The young lady is definitely a looker. But harassing her boyfriend is not the way to a woman's heart, trust me."

Ronin stiffened. "I don't like what you're implying."

Fletcher held up his hands. "I'm not implying anything. And I've no intention of telling you how to do your job." He stood. "I just thought you'd want to know that as far as I've determined, Allerton is clean."

Ronin nodded. "Anything else?"

"No. I'd better be going. I'm seeing a certain school principal this evening." He winked, then strolled out of the office.

Adelaide passed him in the hallway and scowled after him. "When is he going back to Delta, where he belongs?" she asked.

Her obvious dislike for the man surprised Ronin. "Do you have something against Detective Fletcher?" he asked.

"I don't like any man who's so full of himself. Plus—" she lowered her voice "—I have a friend who works with the Colorado Springs PD and she said when Fletcher worked there he was always in trouble for crossing the line in his investigations. A lot of people celebrated when he left there."

"Wait a minute—Jim Fletcher worked for the Colorado Springs PD?"

Adelaide nodded, her cat earrings swaying. "He was on the force there for seventeen years. He worked vice his last three years." She deposited a stack of papers on his desk. "Reports for you to read in your spare time," she said, and left.

If Jim Fletcher had worked for Colorado Springs

PD, why hadn't he known Trey Allerton? Ronin wondered. He would have been working Vice when Trey was questioned in relation to local crimes.

Then again, it was a big department. Maybe he'd been involved in another case at the time.

His conversation with Fletcher had unsettled him. Maybe it was that comment about Courtney. Ronin resented the implication that he would use his position to try to get to a woman. The very idea made him sick to his stomach.

But the kernel of truth in Fletcher's accusation nagged at him, too. He was attracted to Courtney, and if circumstances had been different, he would have asked her out.

But circumstances weren't different. A smart man would accept that and stay away from her.

The problem was, Ronin wasn't feeling very smart these days. And he had a feeling he'd be seeing Courtney again soon. He wanted that to be a good thing, but his instincts told him he might be wrong.

IT WAS WEDNESDAY afternoon before anyone could get free to follow up on Elaine Schaeffer's report of the stolen gold bars. Ronin and Deputy Shane Ellis drove to the Full Moon Mine, Martin Kramer's gold claim, just after one o'clock. The afternoon was clear and bright, the sky an endless expanse of deep blue, the sun bathing the surrounding mountain peaks with a soft light. Another hour or two and conditions would be perfect for photography. Ronin kept a spare camera in his gear bag in his assigned patrol vehicle, but this afternoon he was riding with Shane.

As they passed the trailer where Trey Allerton and Courtney Baker lived, Shane said, "I see they've started construction on Allerton's youth camp. Maybe it's not a big scam after all."

Ronin studied the structures going up behind the trailer at the top of a hill. "Why did you think it was a scam?" he asked.

"For all his talk of wanting to help kids, Trey seemed a lot more focused on hustling money. He always had his hand out."

"Martin Kramer's daughter said her father told her Allerton visited the mine several times. Kramer thought he was snooping around."

"Kramer was paranoid," Shane said. "He thought everyone who pulled into his driveway was there to steal his gold. I'm not saying Allerton wouldn't have liked to get his hand on a box full of gold bars, but everyone thought the only thing Kramer was pulling out of that mine was rocks."

"Then why was Allerton hanging around?" Ronin asked.

"He probably hit Kramer up for a donation."

"Detective Fletcher and I stopped by there yesterday," Ronin said, nodding toward the blue trailer house. "Allerton wasn't there, so we spoke to Courtney."

"How did she look?" Shane asked.

"She looked fine." Not as anxious or tired as she had the first time he'd spotted her, on the side of the road.

"Lauren worries about her," Shane said. "She never

liked Allerton from Day One, but she thinks he's abusing Courtney. She's noticed bruises." He glanced at Ronin. "Courtney says everything is fine, and though I make it a point to keep an eye on her as much as I can, I've never witnessed anything overt."

"I've spoken to her a couple of times when Allerton wasn't around and she's never said anything," Ronin said.

"She's more likely to confide in Lauren than in us. We'll continue to keep an eye on her," Shane said.

That was all they could do for now, Ronin thought. His mother had refused to leave his father for twenty years. She had no money, no job skills, and, as she often claimed, she loved him and didn't want to lose him. Did Courtney feel that way about Trey Allerton? The thought made his stomach twist.

They rode on in silence, the low murmur of the radio and the pop of road gravel against the underside of the SUV providing background for their thoughts.

They came to the sign for the Full Moon Mine and Shane braked for the turn into a drive that was more potholes and ruts than actual driveway. They rocked and bumped up the hill and around a curve, and parked fifty yards from a rough wooden shack with a metal roof. "Home, sweet home," Shane said. "Kramer was either dedicated or demented to live out here by himself."

They climbed out of the vehicle and looked around. The shack was constructed of logs, some with the bark hanging in long strips, stood on end beside each other, the gaps stuffed with mud, moss and what looked like pink fiberglass insulation. Orange rust streaked the metal roof. A blue plastic barrel at one corner of the structure collected what must have been rusty water.

"The mine is up that way." Shane pointed to a rock-lined path that led up a hill, away from the shack. Rusting equipment, relics from the boom days of mining in the area, one hundred years before, lined the path. As they drew closer to the timber frame of the mine entrance, five-gallon plastic buckets of rock were scattered amongst the old ore carts and crossties.

Shane plucked a rock from one of the buckets and hefted it in his hand. "I wonder if there's any gold in here?" he asked.

Ronin selected another rock and studied it. "I'm not sure I know what gold ore looks like," he said. "I don't see anything shiny."

Shane tossed the rock back into the bucket. "Kramer's daughter is going to have her hands full, going through all of this."

"Kramer is claiming self-defense," Ronin said. "If a jury believes him, he'll be coming back here."

They stopped at the entrance to the mine. Full logs framed the opening, with a shed roof jutting out from the rock. A wrought-iron gate that would have covered the entire opening was swung open and rested against the rock the tunnel was bored into. Shane took a large flashlight from his utility belt and switched it on. Ronin did likewise. "Do you know where this strongbox was supposed to be?" Shane asked.

"Kramer's daughter says it's a couple of hundred

yards into the mine, where the tunnel starts to widen out, up near the roof on the right-hand side."

Shane motioned for Ronin to go first. "Let's see what we can find."

The tunnel was narrow, but tall enough to walk down without stooping. Martin Kramer was over six feet tall, so Ronin guessed he had built the tunnels for his own comfort.

The beams of their flashlights illuminated walls of gray rock, shiny with damp, and the smell of wet earth lent the enclosed space a hint of freshness. Every ten feet or so thick timbers framed the tunnel opening.

Two hundred yards in, the tunnel widened into a high-ceilinged room, approximately ten feet across and about that long. Rock littered the space on either side of a three-foot-wide path down the center, from desk-sized boulders to fist-sized chunks. Ronin played the beam of his light along the ceiling, and came to rest on a spot just beneath a timber, and a gaping hole.

"Think that's where the strongbox was?" Shane asked.

"It fits Ms. Schaeffer's description."

The two men moved closer. The hole was at eye level, and less than two feet deep. Shane shone his light along one side. "These look like chisel marks to me," he said. "Pretty fresh. Like someone chiseled the box out of the wall."

"If it was full of gold, it would have weighed a ton," Ronin said. "How did they get it out of here?"

"A wheelbarrow, maybe."

While Shane continued to examine the cavity, Ronin

explored around the room. His light caught the edge of something metallic jutting from a pile of rock. "Shane, come here," he called.

Shane joined him, then reached out and nudged aside a couple of rocks with the toe of his boot. The shape of the metal object was more visible now. "Looks like a strongbox to me," he said.

"The thief must have transferred the gold to something," he said. "Maybe a backpack?"

"We'd better get a crime scene team on this," Shane said. "That metal might have fingerprints."

"A team went over Kramer's shack and the mine after his arrest," Ronin said. "They would have found this."

"We'll have to take another look at their report," Shane said. "But I'm guessing whoever took the contents of the strongbox waited until Kramer was in jail and the place was deserted. They would have had all the time they wanted to search the place and take what they wanted."

"Kramer's daughter didn't mention anything else missing."

"This was probably the only thing in the whole place of much monetary value." Shane kicked at one of the rocks. "Let's get out of here. This place gives me the creeps."

"What do you do with a bunch of gold bars if you have them?" Ronin asked as he followed Shane out of the mine. "It's not like you can pay for your groceries with them at the local market."

"Sell them online?" Shane asked. "Or through some

kind of broker? We'll have to find out. With luck, we'll be able to trace any sellers to our thief."

Shane stopped abruptly and swore. "What is it?" Ronin asked, stopping also and trying to see past his fellow deputy.

Instead of answering, Shane took another few steps forward and wrapped his hand around the iron bars of the gate, which was now blocking the mine entrance.

Ronin stared at the network of bars, not sure of what he was seeing. Shane threw his weight against the gate. It shuddered, but held. Ronin had a memory of a large padlock hanging from the open gate. He keyed the mic on his shoulder. "Unit 8 to Dispatch," he said.

Shane leaned against the gate. "You won't get any reception in here." He looked up, at the granite only inches from their heads. "We're stuck until someone comes looking for us."

Ronin took a deep breath, telling himself to remain calm. "When we don't return to the station or respond to the radio, someone will come looking," he said. They only had a few hours to wait, at most.

"They will," Shane agreed. He looked out through the bars, worry furrowing his normally smooth brow. "Let's just hope they get here before whoever locked us in here gets back."

Chapter Nine

Courtney was hanging sheets on a makeshift clothesline behind the trailer Wednesday afternoon when Detective Fletcher returned. This time he wore a gray sport coat over a peach polo. "Where's Trey?" he asked, when he came around the side of the trailer and saw her—a sharp, abrupt question, without preamble.

She looked past him, hoping to see Ronin, but apparently, the detective was alone. She shifted her gaze back to him. "What do you want with Trey?" she asked.

"I want to talk to him. Now, where is he?"

She debated lying, and telling him she didn't know, but what did it matter, really? If he wanted to talk to Trey, why should she stop him? "He's up at the construction site." She nodded up the hill, where the steady pock! pock! of an air hammer echoed against the surrounding hills.

Fletcher moved past her in long strides that covered ground quickly. She watched him go, sure that was the bulge of a gun beneath the sport coat. As his figure disappeared behind a clump of trees she turned back toward the trailer, then changed her mind and started up the hill after him.

She hadn't visited the construction site since Trey had brought her here the day the work began. Since then, two large wooden platforms had been completed, where canvas tents Trey had purchased from a military surplus store online would be erected. The dining pavilion was almost complete and the outdoor kitchen was taking shape. By next year, Trey had told her, they would add real bunkhouses, a classroom/art room, and restrooms with showers, sinks and toilets. When all that was completed, they would start work on a home for her and Ashlyn and Trey. "The kids come first," he had said, and she had felt a small swell of pride, remembering the early days of discussing this project. They had been so in sync then, about all their goals and plans. It was good to be reminded that at least some of that was still true.

She spotted Fletcher with the two workmen at the corner of the pavilion and moved toward them. "What do you mean you don't know where he went?" Fletcher demanded as she approached.

"I'm working. It's not my job to keep tabs on the boss." The man who spoke was the taller of the two, and he brandished the nail gun like a weapon.

"How long has he been gone?" Fletcher turned to the other, shorter man, who wore a thin moustache that did little to age his baby face.

"Half an hour, maybe?" The shorter man shrugged. Fletcher looked around and spotted Courtney. He strode toward her. "Why didn't you tell me Allerton was gone?" he demanded.

"Because I thought he was up here." She scanned the construction site, but saw no sign of Trey. "He can't have gone far," she said. "His truck is still parked in front of the trailer."

"I'll bet he saw me coming and made himself scarce," Fletcher said.

"Why would he do that?" Courtney asked.

"Because he's a coward," Fletcher said. "He's fine as long as he's dealing with someone weaker than he is."

"Do you and Trey know each other?" she asked, puzzled.

Fletcher glowered. "I know his type." He moved past her, back down the path. She took a last look around and, not spotting Trey, headed back toward the trailer.

Fletcher was waiting by the clothesline, the damp sheets dancing behind him in a sporadic breeze. He clutched her arm when she tried to move past him. "You're in this just as deep as Trey is," he said. "Don't think you aren't."

"I... In what?" She tried to pull away from him, but he only tightened his hold on her.

"Never mind the details," Fletcher said. "Just know that if I find out you've been covering for your boyfriend, I'll come after you, too. Don't forget." He thrust her away from him and left. A few seconds later, she heard a car door slam and an engine start.

By the time she made it back to the trailer, he was gone. Trey's truck was still parked where he had left it when he had returned home yesterday, and except for the dust that still hung in the air from Fletcher's passing, the scene outside was serene and undisturbed.

She sank onto the sofa. She could hear Ashlyn in the next room, singing to herself. She must have awakened from her nap. What had just happened? The detective had seemed agitated, even angry, but was he upset with Trey, or because he couldn't find Trey? Had he seen Fletcher arrive and didn't want to talk to him? But the workman had said he had left a half an hour before.

But where had he gone?

If she had a working phone, she would call Ronin and ask what he thought. Talking to him would make her feel calmer.

Safer, though that idea was a dangerous one. Believing she needed a man to keep her safe had led to her current situation. Though things had been better with Trey lately, and she was thrilled they had begun work on the camp, she no longer wanted to depend on someone else for her safety or happiness.

But she didn't have a phone, or a means of going anywhere, since Trey kept the only set of keys to the truck with him. All she could do was wait—for Trey to return, for Ronin to stop by to see her again, for the rest of her life to begin.

RONIN SAT ON the ground, his back against a boulder, and looked through the photos on his phone. Shane alternated between pacing and staring out between the bars that imprisoned them. "It's been four hours," Shane said. "Someone should be here by now."

"The sheriff assigned us to come here," Ronin said, not for the first time. "He'll send backup to look here first."

"Then why aren't they here?" Shane asked.

"Maybe things got busy and no one has realized yet that we should have returned by now," Ronin said. His stomach growled. He really wished he hadn't skipped lunch.

Shane leaned against the bars. "You don't think Kramer's daughter did this, do you?" he asked. "She lured us out here with her story of a stolen lockbox, then trapped us in here to get back at us for arresting her father?"

"I don't know," Ronin said. "It's a pretty juvenile stunt to pull. She struck me as serious. Maybe it's just teenagers goofing off. They were messing around where they shouldn't be and pulled that gate shut to buy them some time to get away."

"Maybe." Their sense of being in danger had lessened when no one had returned to attack them, replaced by boredom.

Shane slid to the ground and sat, elbows on upraised knees. "I'd kill for a burger and a Coke right now," he said.

"Don't," Ronin said.

"What are you looking at?" Shane asked.

"Photos on my phone. Mostly scenery, quick shots of things I want to return to photograph later." Sometimes he took preliminary crime scene photos with his phone, but those all got uploaded to the department computers and deleted.

He stopped at a photograph of Courtney. He had taken it when he spotted her on the road with her suitcase that first day, a zoomed in shot that showed her in profile, face illuminated by the sun. The image reminded him of a painting by one of the Dutch masters—a beautiful woman bathed in soft light.

He ought to erase the photo. At the time, he had told himself he took it in case something turned out to be wrong, but that was just an excuse. He'd taken it because she was beautiful and something about her—a quality of both strength and vulnerability—drew him.

He swiped to the next shot—an image of storm clouds over the mountains.

"Someone's coming." Shane jumped to his feet and pressed his face to the bars.

Ronin stood also, and pocketed his phone. As he stood beside Shane at the mine entrance, he heard the crunch of tires on gravel.

The vehicle stopped—probably right behind Shane's SUV. After a moment, doors opened. "Shane! Ronin!" Gage Walker's voice echoed in the silence.

"Over here!" Shane shouted. "At the mine." He picked up a rock and began striking the bars of the gate, the percussion hurting Ronin's ears, but it was a sound that would carry further than voices.

A few moments later, footsteps pounded toward them, then Gage appeared, his brother, Sheriff Travis Walker, right behind him.

Gage stopped short of the mine entrance. "How did you two end up in there?" he asked.

"Someone locked us in here," Shane said. "And before you ask, we don't know who. Just get us out of here."

"I've got bolt cutters in the cruiser," Travis said, and turned away.

Gage moved closer. "You two okay otherwise?" he asked.

"We're fine," Ronin said. "We found the empty strongbox. Someone chiseled it out of the wall and emptied the contents. Kramer's daughter said it was full of gold bars."

"While we were back in the mine, someone came up here and closed and padlocked the gate," Shane said.

"But you didn't see or hear anything," Gage said.

"No, we did not."

No one said anything else until Travis returned with the bolt cutters. He cut the lock and removed it with gloved hands and bagged it as evidence.

"Do you think someone followed you here?" Travis asked.

"We didn't see anyone, but they must have," Ronin said.

"Who knew you were coming here?" Gage asked.

"The sheriff," Shane said. "Adelaide. Anyone else who was at the office at the time."

"Someone could have seen us turn onto this road and guessed where we were headed," Ronin said.

"Could have been kids pulling a prank," Gage said.

"You two go back into town," Travis said. "We'll wait here for the crime scene team and have a look around."

"I hope you find more than we did," Shane said. "I think whoever took Kramer's gold is long gone, and so is whoever locked us in there." He rubbed the back of his neck. "What do you think the chances are of keeping this little incident to ourselves?"

Gage grinned. "Pretty much none. This is too good a story not to share. I mean, I wish I'd thought to take a picture of you two looking out past those iron bars. Priceless."

"Thanks a lot," Shane said.

"Come on." Gage clapped him on the shoulder. "If you were in my position, you'd do the same. It's a great story. No one was hurt and you'll be home in time for dinner."

Shane nodded. "It is a good story. And who knows, if we spread it around someone might feel the need to brag that they were the ones to close and lock that gate."

"I like the way you think," Gage said. "Now go on. And tell that crime scene team to hurry. I can guarantee Travis and I aren't going into that tunnel until we have backup."

COURTNEY WAITED UNTIL Trey left Thursday morning before she returned to the storage shed. He'd taken Ashlyn with him, so Courtney was alone. The padlock was back in place, so she bypassed the door and moved around to the back. Unlike a home, with its layers of wood and insulation and wiring and wallboard, only a single sheet of wood siding separated the contents of this shed from the elements. She slipped a tote bag from her shoulder and took out a hammer. She searched along the edge of one sheet of siding until she found a loose nail, then slipped the claw of the hammer beneath it and pulled.

Fifteen minutes later she had succeeded in extracting a dozen nails, enough to pull back the edge of the siding, creating a gap wide enough for her to slip through. But before she could get inside, she had to shove aside the shovel and rake and other tools that hung from that wall. Once those were out of the way, she squeezed in and switched on the flashlight that had also been in her bag.

She went right to the backpack, which was still atop the stack of boxes, and took out two more gold bars. She had no idea how much the gold was worth, but if she and Ashlyn were going to leave and hide from Trey, she'd need money. She could sell the gold for cash to keep them going until she received the next quarterly payment from her trust.

The gold secured, she stopped in front of the trunk and studied it. It was also sealed with a heavy brass padlock. On television, thieves picked locks, but she had no idea how that was done, or if it was even possible with locks like this. She nudged the trunk with her foot, and it slid over an inch. Whatever it contained wasn't that heavy, so it probably wasn't full of gold. It was probably just a bunch of old clothes.

She looked around to check that she hadn't left anything behind, then slipped through the gap in the siding once more.

The bright sun momentarily blinded her, so she

stood for a moment, blinking. The whine of a saw from the construction site up the hill cut the air, and a truck rattled by on the road. She froze at the sound of the vehicle and held her breath until it passed their drive. She caught a glimpse of green through the scrub and relaxed. That was the old green truck that belonged to the couple in the yurt, the Olsens. When she was sure they were well past, she took out the hammer and began nailing the siding in place once more.

Back at the trailer, she retrieved the gold bar she had taken previously from its hiding place in the tampon box and put it and the two others in the bottom of her purse. The weight of it dragged at her shoulder, but she needed to keep the gold close. The first chance she had to leave with Ashlyn, she would have to be ready to go. She would take nothing with her but the purse and her daughter. She had already copied out the phone number of the attorney who handled her trust and put it, along with her and Ashlyn's birth certificates and Social Security cards, into the lining of the purse. She was nervous about leaving. Afraid. But also excited. She felt stronger than she had since Mike had died, more determined to do the right thing, not just the easy thing.

She heard another vehicle approaching and glanced out the front window to see Trey's truck pulling in. She stashed her purse in the bottom drawer of the desk in the corner of the living room, then smoothed her hair and forced a smile to her face.

"Mommy, look what Daddy brought me!" Ashlyn waved a plastic doll.

Courtney's smile vanished, and her stomach hurt. "You mean what Trey brought you," she said, trying to keep her voice gentle. "He's not your daddy."

"I'm as good as a father to her," Trey said. "And it attracts less attention in public if she calls me that."

"Isn't it all right if I call him Daddy?" Ashlyn looked from one to the other, her confusion clear.

It wasn't right, Courtney wanted to shout. Ashlyn had a wonderful father who had died, but Trey was not and never would be her father. "You should call him Trey." She smoothed the hair back from Ashlyn's face, and forced a smile. "That's his name, just like yours is Ashlyn."

"You're not mad at me, are you, Mommy?"

"No! Of course not." She kissed Ashlyn's cheek. "Now show me your dolly." She could feel Trey glaring at her, but she ignored him. She had given in to him about many things, but she wouldn't budge on this one.

He waited until Ashlyn went into her room before he said anything. "What's gotten into you?" he asked.

She forced himself to meet his gaze, not flinching at the anger she saw there. "You're not her father. You're not my husband. It isn't fair to confuse her."

"I'm the only man in either of your lives, so why shouldn't she call me Daddy?"

"Because I don't want her to." She tried not to sound petulant.

Trey slipped his hand along her shoulders to caress the back of her neck, then he gripped hard, hurting her. "Are you getting ideas again, about leaving me?" he asked. "Because it's never going to happen. The only way you can keep your little girl safe is to stay with me. Don't ever forget it."

He shook her, as if he was shaking a disobedient dog, then thrust her away from him. She closed her eyes, willing herself not to give in to the terror. She had no doubt Trey would do everything in his power to keep her with him. Maybe, in his own twisted way, he believed it was because he loved her. He was stronger than she was, and thought he had every advantage.

But she was a mother. She had so much more at stake here, and that made her more powerful than he could ever imagine.

"Hello, Deputy Doyle." Art Stevens looked up from his desk at his office as Ronin entered Thursday morning. "Detective Fletcher isn't with you today?"

"No, I was just passing and thought I'd stop by," Ronin said. He studied a poster on the wall behind Stevens's desk, advertising the Explorer's Club. "Are any of the kids in your group signed up for Trey Allerton's camp, do you know?"

"I believe a couple of them are," Art said. "Trey came and spoke to our group about the camp just a few days ago. He's offering scholarships for kids who might not otherwise be able to afford even his modest fees, and I recommended a couple of boys I thought would particularly benefit. Sometimes a couple of weeks' break from a rough family situation can make all the difference in a kid's life."

"So, you think this Baker Ranch is going to be a good program?" Ronin asked.

"I do. I talked to Trey for quite a while about it, and I even went out and saw the facilities he's building. He's keeping everything simple and rustic at first, but it's very well-thought-out, and I think it's the kind of wholesome activity and individualized attention a lot of kids desperately need."

"Individualized attention?"

"Yes. Trey showed me his staff roster and it comes out to about one staff member for every four kids—a really excellent ratio. And the credentials on the people he has helping him are impressive."

This was the first Ronin had heard of Trey hiring anyone. "Who is he hiring?"

"They're mostly people he worked with in Colorado Springs," Art said. "Teachers, a psychologist, former military people. I haven't met them personally, but they all have a prominent online presence, so it was easy to see the kind of experience they have. The children are going to benefit so much."

"Did you speak to any of them?" Ronin asked. "Ask about their plans for the campers?"

"Well, no, I didn't go that far. But Trey had a whole folder of correspondence with them—emails mostly, but a few letters, also. He's been planning all of this for months and his hard work really shows."

Courtney had mentioned none of this when he had spoken to her last. Why would Trey have kept that from her?

"Did you meet Trey's girlfriend when you visited the camp?" Ronin asked.

"He introduced us briefly," Art said. "A very pretty

young woman. He said she's too busy with their little girl to devote much time to the campers, but I think the fact that he's a father himself will reassure a lot of parents."

"Ashlyn isn't Trey's daughter," Ronin said. "Did he say she was?"

Art flushed. "I just assumed. The way he spoke about the little girl. In any case, I'm sure he's like a father to her." He tilted his head slightly, studying Ronin. "Is something wrong, Deputy? You're asking a lot of questions about that camp. Should I be concerned?"

"I just wanted your professional opinion, as someone who has a lot of experience working with young people," Ronin said. "A friend is interested."

"Oh." Stevens relaxed. "I think the best thing would be for your friend to contact Mr. Allerton and talk to him. He was very open with me."

"I'll do that," Ronin said. He started to move toward the door.

"Before you go, Deputy, would you be interested in speaking to our group? We're always looking for people to give interesting presentations."

"Do you really think they'd be interested in hearing from a cop?" Ronin asked.

Stevens grinned. "Actually, Detective Fletcher has agreed to come and talk about his police work. I thought you could talk about photography, maybe show some of your work. I know several of our teens are interested in photography."

"Sure. I could talk to them."

"What about next month? The first Saturday at

11:00 a.m.? We can't pay you, but you'll be doing something good for the kids."

Ronin nodded. "I'd be happy to."

"Wonderful. I'll send out a reminder the week before, so you don't forget."

From Stevens's office it was a short walk to the Pear Tree Gallery, where his showing would open on Saturday. The owner, Maydelle Hastings, greeted him with a smile. "We've had a wonderful response to the postcards I sent out about your show," she said. "We should have a good turnout. I hope you're looking forward to it."

He was and he wasn't. As much as he enjoyed taking photographs and sharing them with others, it meant opening himself up to criticism. Maydelle correctly interpreted his expression. "It's natural to be nervous, but you'll do fine," she said. "And I'm anticipating a good sell-through, also. Otherwise, I wouldn't have invited you to have a showing."

"No pressure," he said.

She laughed again. "None at all. You don't have anything to worry about."

Nothing except a murdered teenager, a missing cache of gold bars, and his attraction to a woman who was involved with a man who kept showing up as a suspect in criminal cases.

He left the gallery and headed back to where he had parked his sheriff's department SUV. As he passed an alley, movement in the shadows caught his eye and he stopped to look. Detective Fletcher was in heated conversation with a man who was deeper in shadow.

He couldn't hear what Fletcher was saying, but his expression was one of anger, and he was pointing a finger at the other man, whose face Ronin couldn't make out. "Is everything all right, Detective?" Ronin called.

Fletcher jerked his head up, then planted his hand flat against the other man's chest, as if to hold him back. "Everything's fine, Deputy," he called. "Just having a private conversation."

Ronin got the impression Fletcher was annoyed by the interruption, so he nodded and moved on. But he sat in his SUV for a moment, watching in the rearview mirror until Fletcher emerged, alone, from the alley. The detective glanced toward Ronin's vehicle, then turned and headed the opposite direction.

Ronin remained parked, waiting for the other man to emerge. But instead of a man, a little girl leaned out from the alley. With a start, Ronin recognized Ashlyn Baker. She stared at his SUV, then disappeared back into the alley.

Ronin got out of the vehicle and walked back to the alley. "Ashlyn?" he called.

No answer came, and nothing stirred in the shadows. Every nerve on edge, Ronin moved cautiously into the alley. "Ashlyn?" he called again.

No answer. He walked the length of the alley, to the edge of the brick wall that blocked its far end. He looked behind the trash cans outside the doors of the businesses that opened onto the space, and tried both doors, which were locked.

If Ashlyn was here, did that mean Trey Allerton

was here, too? "Trey!" Ronin shouted. "Trey Allerton, I need to talk to you."

Silence.

Ashlyn—and the man Fletcher had been talking to—had vanished.

Chapter Ten

Taking and hiding the gold made Courtney feel powerful and brave. Trey would be furious if he found out, but she intended to be gone before that happened, and this time she would take Ashlyn with her.

How to get away when she had no car and no way to call anyone, and how to escape without involving an innocent person whom Trey might come to blame still eluded her. But she was determined to take any opportunity that presented itself.

Friday when Trey left, he didn't take Ashlyn with him. The little girl spilled her milk at breakfast and hid in her room when it was time for Trey to leave. She refused to go with him and kicked and screamed when he tried to pick her up. "I don't have time for this," he declared, and stalked out of the room and out of the house.

When he was gone, Courtney sat on the floor beside Ashlyn. "What's wrong?" she asked. "Are you not feeling well?"

"I hate it here," Ashlyn said. "Why can't we live somewhere else?"

Why not, indeed? "Let's get you dressed and I'll fix your hair and we'll walk up and see the construction workers," she said.

"I don't want to," Ashlyn said. She sniffed and scrubbed at her nose.

"It's a pretty day out, and it will be good to take a walk," Courtney said. "I don't want to go by myself, so please come with me."

The pleading, and Courtney's agreement to let Ashlyn wear her favorite dress—pink with a tulle skirt—improved the toddler's temper.

Half an hour later, Ashlyn ran ahead of Courtney up the path behind the trailer to where a trio of buildings were taking shape. Two men stood on scaffolding at the side of one building, nailing roof trusses into place. Trey had referred to them as Ed and Bert, a father-and-son team he had hired from Olathe.

"Hello!" Courtney called, and waved.

The older of the two—Ed—set down a nail gun and squinted down at her. "Hello, Mrs. Allerton," he said, his manner very formal.

She wanted to argue that she wasn't married to Trey, but resisted the urge. Trey had mentioned that the two men belonged to some fundamentalist religious sect—she couldn't recall which. But maybe they would think she and Trey living together was terribly sinful, and she needed them to like her.

"I'm sorry to bother you," she said. "But I was wondering if I could borrow your truck. My little girl is sick and I need to get her to the doctor."

Ed looked toward the mustard yellow pickup parked

in the thin shade of a pinon nearby. Then his gaze shifted to Ashlyn, who squatted in the dirt, arranging cutoff pieces of two-by-fours into patterns. "You want me to lend you my truck?" he asked, as if he must not have heard her correctly.

"Yes. I promise to bring it back as soon as the doctor has seen Ashlyn. She's running a high fever and I'm really worried." The lies came effortlessly, and some other time she might have blushed at her sudden talent for deception. But she didn't have time for analysis, or guilt. She was desperate to get away while she had the chance.

Ed scratched his beard. Bert came to stand beside his father, a clean-shaven, younger version of the older man, with matching denim overalls and long-sleeved blue work shirt. "Mr. Allerton said we weren't to talk to you," Ed said.

"Then give me the keys and I'll go now," she said, trying to disguise her impatience.

Ed's gaze returned to Ashlyn. "The little girl looks all right to me," he said. "Why don't you wait until Mr. Allerton gets home? If he thinks she needs a doctor, he can take her."

"I don't know when he'll be home," she said. "I really do need to take her now."

Ed shook his head. "I can't let you take the truck. If Mr. Allerton found out, he would fire us."

"He's more likely to reward you for helping to take care of his little girl." This lie was harder to deliver, but maybe her agitation would convince this man that she was desperate.

Ed picked up the air hammer. "Best to wait until your husband gets home," he said.

The younger man, Bert, cleared his throat. "Why don't you use the Toyota?" he asked.

"The Toyota?" Courtney looked around. The only vehicle visible was the truck, a Ford.

"In the shed." Bert gestured behind him.

Courtney took Ashlyn's hand and led the little girl around the side of the building under construction. After a few seconds, the nail gun began firing again.

The shed was another new structure, tucked behind a cluster of trees, so that it wasn't readily visible from elsewhere on the property. Once the unpainted siding weathered to gray, the building would be practically invisible. She hadn't even known it was here. If she had noticed it, she would have assumed it was part of the new camp.

No lock secured the double doors that filled most of the front of the shed. Courtney tugged on one door and it swung open smoothly.

Sunlight slanted through the opening onto the dirt floor and a white Toyota Rav4 taking up most of the space.

Her Toyota. The one Trey had persuaded her to sell.

"Why is our car here, Mommy?" Ashlyn asked.

"I don't know, honey." She ran her hand over the edge of the hood. Three weeks ago she had signed the back of the title and Trey had promised to take care of everything else.

She had believed at least part of the money going

Get ready to relax and indulge with your FREE BOOKS and more!

Claim up to FOUR NEW BOOKS & TWO MYSTERY GIFTS – absolutely FREE!

Dear Reader,

We both know life can be difficult at times. That's why it's important to treat yourself so you can relax and recharge once in a while.

And I'd like to help you do this by sending you this amazing offer of up to FOUR brand new full length FREE BOOKS that WE pay for.

This is everything I have ready to send to you right now:

Try **Harlequin® Romantic Suspense** books featuring heart-racing page-turners with unexpected plot twists and irresistible chemistry that will keep you guessing to the very end.

Try **Harlequin Intrigue® Larger-Print** books featuring action-packed stories that will keep you on the edge of your seat. Solve the crime and deliver justice at all costs.

Or **TRY BOTH!**

All we ask in return is that you answer 4 simple questions on the attached Treat Yourself survey. You'll get **Two Free Books** and **Two Mystery Gifts** from each series you try, *altogether worth over $20*! Who could pass up a deal like that?

Sincerely,

Pam Powers

Harlequin Reader Service

Treat Yourself to Free Books and Free Gifts.

Answer 4 fun questions and get rewarded.

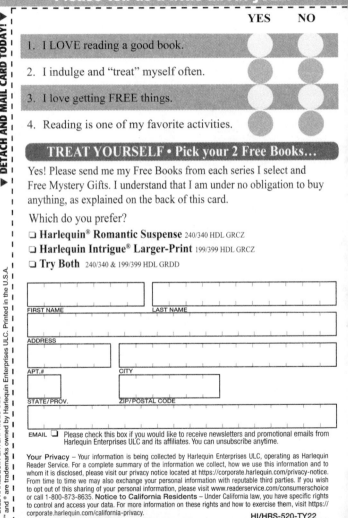

▶ DETACH AND MAIL CARD TODAY! ▶

	YES	NO
1. I LOVE reading a good book.		
2. I indulge and "treat" myself often.		
3. I love getting FREE things.		
4. Reading is one of my favorite activities.		

TREAT YOURSELF • Pick your 2 Free Books...

Yes! Please send me my Free Books from each series I select and Free Mystery Gifts. I understand that I am under no obligation to buy anything, as explained on the back of this card.

Which do you prefer?

☐ **Harlequin® Romantic Suspense** 240/340 HDL GRCZ
☐ **Harlequin Intrigue® Larger-Print** 199/399 HDL GRCZ
☐ **Try Both** 240/340 & 199/399 HDL GRDD

FIRST NAME   LAST NAME

ADDRESS

APT.#   CITY

STATE/PROV.   ZIP/POSTAL CODE

EMAIL ☐ Please check this box if you would like to receive newsletters and promotional emails from Harlequin Enterprises ULC and its affiliates. You can unsubscribe anytime.

HI/HRS-520-TY22

into building the camp had come from the sale of her SUV—yet here it sat. Why?

She tried to open the driver's door, but it was locked. She had turned over her keys along with the title, which meant Trey must have them now. If she could find them, she could drive away from here, as far as she wanted to go. Back to her old life in Denver, or to a new life somewhere else. Her heart fluttered with excitement.

She looked around the shed for any hiding place where Trey might have stashed the key, but the rest of the space was empty. Nothing hung from nails on the bare studs that lined the walls and there were no shelves or niches or storage containers. Just a shed, perhaps purpose-built to hide this vehicle. But again—why?

She felt around the frame of the vehicle, hoping to find one of those magnetic boxes people sometimes used to hide a spare key. But there was nothing under there but dried mud.

"Mommy, I'm thirsty," Ashlyn said. "Can we go back to the house and get a drink?"

"Sure, honey." Courtney wiped her hands on her jeans, then led Ashlyn out of the shed, and shut the door behind her. She headed up to the road and walked back to the trailer that way to avoid Ed and Bert.

Back home, she fed Ashlyn lunch, then searched every inch of the trailer for the Toyota key. She found a pistol she hadn't known about, some canned goods she had forgotten she bought, and a good bit of lint and dust, but no key.

By the time Trey returned at five she was tired and sweaty, and furious.

But she couldn't ask him about the Toyota in front of Ashlyn, so she had to wait until the little girl was fed, bathed and put to bed.

Trey was in an odd mood. He followed Courtney from room to room, and every time she looked up from whatever she was doing, he was staring at her. "What's wrong?" she asked, the third time she caught him watching her. "What are you looking at?"

He shook his head, and turned his attention back to his book, but when she glanced up a fourth time, he was glaring at her again.

Early in their relationship, he would have teased or flirted, or made some excuse that he couldn't keep his eyes off her. She'd been flattered. Before she started dating Mike she hadn't gone out with very many men. She was an only child and her parents were very strict, not allowing her to date until she was seventeen, and then only agreeing to let her go out with boys from their church.

She was nineteen when she met Mike. Her parents hadn't been sure of him at first, but he had won them over with his good manners and clean-cut good looks. The fact that he was in the military gave him the ultimate stamp of approval and they had approved of the marriage. *I know you'll take good care of our girl*, her father had told Mike shortly after the engagement.

When Mike had been deployed less than a year after the wedding, Courtney had been alone for the first time in her life. She'd gotten through those first lonely months by focusing on a future when they would be together again. Then Ashlyn had been born and Courtney's hours were filled with caring for a baby.

Some women would have turned to their mother for help, but Courtney didn't have that kind of relationship with her parents. Two months after her wedding they had moved to China to serve as missionaries. It was as if they had decided they had done their duty, Courtney was taken care of, so they could focus on other things. Courtney received the occasional letter and that was all.

After Mike's death, with Ashlyn a little older, Courtney had been hit with the realization that this could be the rest of her life—raising a child by herself, with no one else to rely on.

Now, with the wisdom of hindsight, she realized there were worse fates than being alone. She missed making her own decisions and charting her own course. She missed feeling safe in her own home.

When she was sure Ashlyn was asleep, Courtney returned to the living room. "I walked up to see the construction today," she said.

"You did?" Trey looked up from the magazine he was reading. "You really shouldn't go up there while Ed and Bert are working. It could be dangerous."

"Why did you tell them not to talk to me?"

"I'm paying them to work, not talk. Besides, it's not as if you'd want to make friends with those two." He laid aside the magazine. "Is that what has you so upset? You've been looking at me like I shot your dog all afternoon."

"What has me upset is that you talked me into letting you sell my car, and it's been sitting in a shed out there all this time." She pointed in the direction of the construction. "I found the shed, and I found my Toyota in it."

"I did sell it," he said, his expression bland. "The owner asked me to keep it for a few weeks. He wants to surprise his daughter on her birthday."

"And you didn't bother to tell me this before?"

"I know how much it hurt to part with your car," he said. "I didn't think it was worth upsetting you."

"Well, I'm upset now."

He spread his hands wide. "I don't know what you want me to do."

"Tell the buyer I've changed my mind. Tell him the deal is off. I want my car back. It's not safe, not having my own transportation when you're away so much."

"The title has already been transferred," he said. "It's too late."

"Then we'll buy another car. You can take me to get it tomorrow."

"Now, Courtney." He stood. "Don't be unreasonable."

She backed away from him. "No. You're the one who's being unreasonable. I want my own car again."

"There's no sense discussing this while you're so agitated," he said. He sat and picked up the magazine again.

She glared at him. She wanted to throw something at him, to force him to pay attention to her. But that never worked with Trey. Sometimes she thought the way he had of dismissing her like this was worse than when he hit her.

"I'm going to bed," she said.

"You do that. Maybe tomorrow you'll wake up in a better mood."

She went to bed, sure she would spend the night tossing and turning, reliving their argument in her head. But instead, she fell quickly asleep.

She didn't know how much time had passed when Trey shook her awake. She opened her eyes to darkness, his face a shadowy blur as he bent over her. "Get up and get dressed," he ordered.

She sat up and shook her head, trying to shrug off sleep. "What is it?" she asked. "What's wrong?"

"Never mind that. Get dressed."

She switched on the lamp and stared at him. He was wearing the same jeans and black T-shirt he'd had on yesterday, but his hair was a wild tangle, as if he had repeatedly run his fingers through it. He moved with frantic, jerky motions and his voice when he spoke was sharp and impatient. "Get up!" he ordered.

She swung her legs to the side of the bed and stood and went into the bathroom. Trey followed. "Hurry up," he said.

She deliberately took her time brushing her teeth, watching him in the mirror as she worked. He looked angry, but also a little afraid. She started to ask him again what was wrong, then decided to get dressed first. She felt less vulnerable when she had more clothes on.

She dressed in jeans, a long-sleeved T-shirt, and tennis shoes. While she was putting on her clothes, Trey left. A few moments later, she heard Ashlyn wailing.

Courtney ran to Ashlyn's room and found Trey holding the girl by both arms, dangling her over the bed. "What are you doing?" Courtney demanded. "Put her down."

Trey let go and Ashlyn crumpled to the bed, wailing even louder. "Get her dressed," Trey said.

Courtney pulled her daughter closer. For the first time since he had awakened her, she looked at a clock. Four thirty! "Have you been up all night?" she asked, alarmed.

"It's your fault!" he snapped, and went into the other room.

She managed to calm Ashlyn and get her dressed, then wrapped her in a blanket and carried her into the living room. "Let's go," Trey said, and took out his keys.

"Not until you tell me what's going on," Courtney said.

Trey glared at her, his jaw moving. Was he grinding his teeth? "You want to know what's wrong. This is what's wrong!" He jerked open the bottom drawer of the desk and pulled out her purse, which he up-ended, spilling the contents across the carpet. Her wallet, phone, tissues, makeup and snacks—they all cascaded onto the carpet. Trey shook the purse and the gold bars tumbled out—one, two, three, landing with a soft thud! thud! thud!

Courtney bit the inside of her cheek, fighting a wave of terror-induced nausea. "Did you think I wouldn't find out you've been stealing from me?" He grabbed her arm and shook her, the way he had shaken the purse. Ashlyn began to wail and Courtney tried to comfort the heavy, sleepy child.

Trey kept his grip on her and leaned in, his face close enough she could feel his hot breath and smell its sourness. "You were planning to leave me, weren't you?" he said.

"N…no," she lied.

He swore and shook her again, so that her head snapped back and her teeth rattled. Ashlyn's screams rose, hurting Courtney's ears.

"I told you I wasn't going to let that happen," Trey said. "Shut up!" He hit Ashlyn, his hand leaving a red mark on her cheek. The little girl stared at him in horror, then buried her face against Courtney's shoulder, her whole body shaking with silent sobs.

"You keep your hands off of her!" Courtney shouted, enraged. She tried to squirm out of his grasp, but he only tightened his grip and dragged her toward the door.

"Let's go," he said.

She held back, dragging her feet. "Where are you taking us?" she demanded.

"Somewhere safe," he said. "Where you won't get away."

Chapter Eleven

Ronin settled on a blue button-down and newer jeans to wear to his gallery show that Saturday. As he ran a brush through his hair he thought it would be good to have a wife or girlfriend who could have passed judgment on his appearance. One of the advantages of wearing a uniform most days was that he didn't have to make these kinds of decisions.

He arrived at the gallery at ten thirty and walked around the empty space, pretending to study the display of his work and trying not to appear too anxious. When the bell on the front door sounded, relief flooded him as the sheriff stepped inside, with his wife, Lacy, and Shane Ellis and Lauren Baker.

"Thanks for coming," Ronin said, hurrying over to greet them.

"We've been looking forward to it." Lacy Walker, an attractive brunette who was obviously pregnant, surveyed the wall of framed photos. "Your work is so beautiful."

"Lauren thinks we have too many blank walls in our

place," Shane said. "We thought we'd buy something so we can say we knew you when."

"I wish Courtney would come see this," Lauren said. "She's always loved landscapes, and yours are so beautiful."

"I invited her," Ronin said. "But she said she couldn't make it." Better not to go into detail.

Lauren's expression grew troubled. "She only does what Trey wants her to do," she said. "He talked her into selling her SUV, so now she has to rely on him if she wants to go anywhere."

"There are other one-car families who find a way to make it work," Shane said.

"They're not miles from town with no phone," Lauren said. She glanced at Ronin and softened her voice. "Sorry. I never have liked Trey Allerton, so I tend to get worked up about him."

Another group of people entered, and Ronin moved to greet them.

An hour later, the small gallery was packed with people. Ronin had sold three pieces. Lacy Walker had purchased a scene of a sunset over Dakota Ridge, while Shane and Lauren chose a photo of a weathered barn against a stormy sky.

Adelaide arrived at the end of that first hour, her purple-framed bifocals matching her purple leggings and the purple irises on her quilted black tunic. "It's good to see all your talent isn't wasted taking crime scene photos," she told Ronin when she found him near the buffet table at the back of the room. She indicated a grouping of photos nearest them. "Where did you take these? I thought I knew every set of mine ruins in the county and I don't recognize them."

"It's part of the settlement above the Sanford Mine," he said. The trio of photos depicted the remains of three cabins, all in various stages of decay, the last little more than a foundation and a few logs. "It's quite a hike up that ridge, off the main trail a ways. I found them by accident when I was hoping to get some shots looking down on the surviving mine buildings. I don't think a lot of people make it up there."

"Well, they're striking." Adelaide helped herself to a cup of punch.

"I want to go up there again," Ronin said. "Maybe in the fall, or after a frost."

Adelaide set her half-filled cup aside. "Excuse me, Deputy," she said, and sidled away.

Ronin turned to see what had startled her and was surprised to see Detective Fletcher working his way through the crowd. "Why are you hiding back here, Doyle?" Fletcher said when he reached Ronin.

"Just taking a break," Ronin said. "Would you like something to eat or drink?"

"No thanks. I just stopped by to make sure you didn't misunderstand what I was doing in that alley the other day. I was just having a little discussion with a man who'd been giving Susan a hard time. We stepped into the alley because it didn't seem like a good idea to be discussing a private matter in the street."

"Who was the guy?" Ronin asked.

"Just a parent. He said some things to Susan that made her feel a little threatened. I let him know I wouldn't stand for that and he backed down real quick. It's all good now."

"I thought I saw Ashlyn Baker come out of that alley after you left," Ronin said.

"Who?"

"The daughter of Courtney Baker—Trey Allerton's girlfriend."

Fletcher laughed. "Maybe you've been working too hard. There was no one else in that alley." He clapped his hand on Ronin's shoulder. "I have to go now. See you around."

He pushed his way back through the crowd, straight for the door. He hadn't even glanced at the photographs.

Travis joined Ronin by the refreshment table. "Everything okay?" he asked. "Fletcher left in a hurry."

Ronin debated telling the sheriff about Fletcher in the alley with someone Ronin couldn't see, and the appearance, and then disappearance, of Ashlyn Baker. But there was no law against someone talking in the alley. And he had no proof that Fletcher had been talking to Trey Allerton. He needed to do a little more digging on his own.

"I talked to Fletcher briefly yesterday afternoon," Travis said. "He said the other missing boy has been found, staying with friends."

"That's good," Ronin said. "Anything new on the boy whose body we found?"

"Nothing. Fletcher told me at least one of their witnesses who said Bart Smith was operating from a ranch here has changed his statement, and Fletcher's investigation has turned up nothing."

"Funny that Fletcher didn't mention it just now," Ronin said.

"I told him we'd be alert for anyone who seemed focused on local teens. So far, there's been no uptick in local drug traffic."

"Let's hope that doesn't happen," Ronin said. "Any leads on Martin Kramer's missing gold?"

"Nothing," Travis said. "That's something you can focus on next week. Meanwhile, good luck with the rest of the show. It looks like Lacy's ready to leave."

Lacy, her purchase in hand, waved from near the door. Ronin followed the sheriff and thanked her.

"It's a great turnout, Ronin." Maydelle moved to his side and patted his arm. "You should be very pleased."

"I am. Thanks for giving me this opportunity."

"I'm always pleased to showcase local talent. You have a good eye. I imagine that comes in handy in your law enforcement work."

"Hmm." He didn't think he was any better than any other officer at seeing the potential for crime or uncovering clues others didn't see, but he had no interest in debating the point.

By two o'clock, the crowd had dwindled. The refreshments had mostly vanished and Ronin had made another sale. "There will be more sales," Maydelle said. "We'll leave the rest of your work up until the end of the month. Some of the people who were here today will come back for another look, and other people will stop by who couldn't be here for the reception. But you did well."

Ronin was pleased with the results. The show had

already netted him a tidy sum, which he would probably end up spending on more photography equipment.

He drove home and changed, but was too restless to settle down, so he grabbed his photography bag and went for a drive.

He ended up on County Road 361, and drove slowly past Courtney and Trey's trailer. Trey's truck was parked out front, but there was no sign of anyone outside, and the blinds on the windows were drawn. The construction site up the hill was empty and silent.

He parked at the trailhead for the Sanford Mine and hiked up, past the mine to the ridge with the remains of the three cabins. A hundred years ago single men and families had lived in these one-room log structures, eight foot on a side with walls chinked with mud and moss and an iron stove for heat. One of the cabins still contained the rusting remains of a stove, while a second held what was left of a set of bedsprings, the bed small by today's standards.

He took a dozen photos, then moved up the hill, looking for more ruins, or a different angle on this grouping.

Something shiny in the undergrowth caught his attention. He moved closer and was startled to find a door cut into the side of a hill. The brightness that had caught his eye was from a brass padlock affixed to a new-looking hasp on the door.

Who would put a new lock on a door amid ruins like this? he wondered.

He raised his camera and studied the scene through the viewfinder. He snapped off a few shots, then lowered the camera and considered the scene not as a photographer, but as a cop.

His supposition that the lock was a recent addition was bolstered by fresh scraping in the dirt around the door, as if whoever was using it had to clear away dirt and plants in order to open the door.

The door opening appeared to have been chiseled from the rock, then fitted with a wooden door cut especially to fit from slabs of logs bound together with iron straps. There were no windows, and the roof was so covered in moss and draped over with vines it was almost invisible.

Ronin's uneasiness grew as he studied the structure. He should probably leave. If he got into trouble up here, out of cell phone range, he had no way to summon help. He took a few more pictures, started to turn away, then froze. Had that noise come from inside the structure?

He put his hand on the gun in the holster on his hip. "Hello?" he called. "Is someone there?"

"Ronin! Ronin, is that you?"

"Who is it?"

"It's Courtney. And Ashlyn. Oh, Ronin, you have to help us."

BEING LOCKED IN that cave, underground in complete darkness, was like being buried alive. Courtney had fought with everything she had to keep Trey from shoving her in there, but he had hit her so hard she had almost blacked out, and in that time he had pushed her into that underground room, and tossed a screaming Ashlyn in after her.

Ashlyn had been hysterical when the darkness closed around them. Courtney fought down her own panic to try to calm the child. She pulled Ashlyn into her lap and held her tightly, both of them wrapped in the blanket from Ashlyn's room. When talking didn't help, she sang to the girl—every nursery song and lullaby she could remember, until her voice was hoarse. The singing helped her, too. It kept her from thinking about what else might be in this darkness with them.

After a while, as her eyes grew more accustomed to the darkness, she realized a little light seeped in around the edges of the door. She moved over to sit with her back against the rough wood. When Trey came back— and she prayed that he would come back, that he hadn't left them here to starve in the darkness—she would be ready. She would fight her way out of here by whatever means was necessary.

When she heard someone moving around on the other side of the door, she thought it was Trey. But whoever it was moved away. Terrified she would miss her chance to be saved, she pounded on the door and called out. "Help! Help!"

"Hello? Is someone there?"

Ronin! She sobbed with relief. "It's Courtney! And Ashlyn! Ronin, you have to help us."

He tugged on the door, but it scarcely moved. "I'm going to have to shoot the lock off," he said. "You need to move as far away from the door as you can."

"All right." She picked up Ashlyn and began backing up, one arm stretched out behind her to feel for the wall, her feet dragging on the uneven ground. She estimated she had traveled about eight feet when her hand encountered rough stone. "We're all the way back!" she shouted.

"Turn around and cover your eyes!" he ordered.

She did as he asked, shielding Ashlyn with her body. "Put your hands over your ears," she told her daughter, and moved Ashlyn's hands into place. Then she hunched over the little girl, crouched against the back wall.

Even though she was expecting the gunfire, the loud report startled a scream from her. Ashlyn screamed, too, then began to wail, her little body trembling in terror.

"It's okay." Courtney hugged her close and tried to comfort her. "It's going to be all right."

She looked over her shoulder and the beam of a flashlight momentarily blinded her, then the beam moved to the side and Ronin was there, gathering her and Ashlyn into his arms. "Thank God I found you," he said.

"We have to get out of here before Trey comes back," Courtney said.

"I can carry Ashlyn," he said, but the little girl shrank back against Courtney, her eyes wide.

"I'd better take her," Courtney said. "This has been awful for her."

"Of course." He took Courtney's arm and guided her gently through the door, into the soft light of late afternoon.

Tears streamed down her face. "I thought we were going to die in there," she said, and began to sob.

Ronin gathered them close again. Ashlyn was crying now, too, and he patted her shoulder and stroked Courtney's hair. "You're both safe with me now. It's going to be okay."

His fingers brushed the tender place where Trey had hit her and she flinched. He drew back, frowning, then leaned in to examine the tender lump at her temple. "Did Trey do this?"

"Yes. I'd have never gone in that…that tomb if he hadn't."

"You can tell me what happened later," Ronin said. "For now, let's get out of here."

"Yes."

"I'm parked at the trailhead," he said. "It's about two and a half miles."

"I don't care how far it is, as long as we'll be safe at the end of it."

She would have thought she could have run to her freedom, but the reality of carrying a toddler down a steep, ill-defined trail made that impossible. Before they had gone far at all, Ronin persuaded Ashlyn to let him carry her.

"I promise I'll be right here," Courtney assured the girl.

They made faster progress after that, but it still took the better part of an hour to hike the two and a half miles. Whether it was the blow to her head or the strain of the past twelve hours, Courtney fought waves of nausea and dizziness that made her want to lie down right there on the ground and curl into a ball. But she forced herself to keep going, stumbling at times, but determined to remain on her feet. Ronin stopped every few hundred yards to wait for her to catch up. Once he insisted they all stop and drink some water, and he found a protein bar in his pack and gave it to Ashlyn. He offered Courtney a second bar, but she refused.

"When we get to town, we'll call Lauren and Shane," he said.

"That sounds like a good idea." Lauren was someone she and Ashlyn both loved and trusted.

They set out walking again. The trail wasn't as steep here, and Courtney tried to distract herself from her physical discomfort by focusing on the beautiful scenery around her. Lichen and moss painted colorful patterns on granite boulders beside the trail, and the white trunks of aspen stood like stately pillars on either side of the path. The aspen leaves rustled like taffeta skirts in the breeze and birds trilled like an orchestra warming up for a performance.

"We're almost there," Ronin said after a while. Sweat made a dark stain on the back of his shirt. He must be worn-out, carrying Ashlyn and his camera equipment, but he hadn't slowed his pace except to allow Courtney to catch up.

The sight of his Jeep was like a shot of adrenaline, and her steps grew lighter and quicker, but before they left the shelter of the trees, Ronin stopped and put out a hand to halt her progress. "Something isn't right," he said softly.

He pushed Ashlyn into her arms, then drew his gun. "Wait here," he said.

She tried to look past him, but the squirming child made it impossible to see. By the time she had settled the toddler on her hip, Ronin had moved toward the parked vehicle.

Her gaze shifted from him to the Jeep. At first, she didn't see anything wrong, then she realized that both tires she could see from here were flat.

Ronin reached the vehicle, and frowned down at the slumped tires. He walked all the way around the vehicle, then stood for several minutes, scanning the area. Finally, he motioned for Courtney to join him.

"What happened to your tires?" she asked when she reached his side.

"They've been slashed," he said. "All four of them, plus the spare."

"Who would do something so awful?" she asked.

"I can think of one person."

Trey. She swallowed past the knot of fear that formed in her throat. "Do you think Trey did this?" she asked.

But Ronin had moved away from her. He took out his key fob and pressed the button to unlock the vehicle.

Glass exploded as gunfire blasted. Ronin shoved Courtney hard to the ground. Her knees hit the dirt, then she was sprawling, Ashlyn beneath her, Ronin on top of her. He shoved her half-beneath the vehicle, then crouched on one knee to fire into the woods across from them.

The Jeep shook as bullets raked the side. Courtney's ears rang, and her head throbbed. Ashlyn lay still beneath her, breathing heavily but not making a sound.

She couldn't believe this was happening. Yes, Trey

had been behaving oddly, and he treated her more like a possession than a loved one, but why would he lash out like this now? The idea enraged her. She levered herself up on her elbows. "Why don't you go away and leave us alone!" she shouted. "Don't be an idiot!"

She'd expected another blast of gunfire, but her only answer was silence.

"Mama, you're hurting me," Ashlyn whimpered.

Courtney sat up, taking her weight off the girl. "I'm sorry," she said, and hugged the child close.

"Why is someone shooting at us?" Ashlyn asked. Courtney was relieved to see that the child looked less dazed and terrified.

"I don't know," she said.

Ronin moved to kneel beside her, though he continued to scan the woods. "Do you think he's gone?" Courtney asked.

He shook his head. "He was waiting here for us. Or at least, he was waiting for me. He's seen this vehicle before, so he would know it was mine."

"Why would he shoot at you?" Courtney asked.

"I don't know. And I don't know why he's stopped now, unless it's to come at us from another angle." He touched her shoulder. "It isn't safe, staying here."

That seemed obvious, though leaving the shelter of the Jeep didn't seem very wise, either. "What are we going to do?" she asked.

"I think—"

But she didn't get to hear what he thought. Somewhere nearby, a car engine roared to life. Then the sound began to move toward them.

"He left to get his vehicle," Ronin said. He stood, then pulled her up beside him. "We've got to leave before he gets back," he said.

"Yes."

He stooped over Ashlyn. "I need to carry you again, okay?"

She looked to Courtney, who nodded. "Let Ronin carry you, honey. Please."

Ashlyn held up her arms, and when Ronin scooped her up, she wrapped her arms around his neck.

"Come on," Ronin said to Courtney. "We've got to move fast."

Then he led the way back into the woods, jogging to put as much distance as possible between themselves and a man who wanted to kill them.

Chapter Twelve

Ronin had a stitch in his side, and his thigh ached where Ashlyn's shoe bounced against him. His head throbbed and tension had the back of his neck in a vise.

"Where are we going?" Courtney gasped, half stumbling over the rough terrain. They'd started out on the trail, which had allowed them to move quickly, but after the first mile he had led them off to the side. He'd pulled out his phone and used the compass app to plot a course that he hoped would eventually lead back to the road. If they could reach the Olsens' yurt they could get help.

Ronin stopped and waited for her to catch up with him. He showed her the phone. "If we keep heading roughly southwest, we should come to the Olsens' property," he said.

She squinted at the screen. "Okay. If you say so."

"Mommy, I have to pee," Ashlyn said.

Ronin hoped he didn't look as alarmed as that statement made him feel, but the laughter that briefly lightened Courtney's expression told him she had read him like a book. "Let her down and I'll take her to use the bathroom," she said.

"Don't go far," he said, and lowered the child to the ground.

"We'll just go over here behind this big tree."

While they took care of business, he made a quick inventory of the contents of his pack—two more protein bars, a little over a liter of water, a fleece jacket, knit cap and gloves, some matches and some first aid supplies. And his camera equipment, which was heavy, but he wasn't yet desperate enough to leave it behind. Courtney and Ashlyn had a blanket between them.

She returned to his side with Ashlyn. "Have some water," he said, and handed her the bottle.

"How far are we from the Olsens?" she asked after she and Ashlyn had finished the water.

"My best guess is about five miles. Maybe more if we have to make many detours."

Her eyes widened, then she glanced overhead. "It's getting dark."

"I keep watching the phone, hoping we'll catch a signal."

"That would be nice, but we can't depend on it," she said.

"No." And their chances of getting lost, or injured in a fall, increased as the light dimmed. "We may have to spend the night out here."

It was his turn to read her thoughts on her face, but all she said was, "I haven't camped outside since I was a kid."

He glanced at the phone again. "Let's see how far we can get before dark."

They didn't get far. Ashlyn refused to let Ronin or

her mother carry her, but when left to walk on her own, she dragged her feet, or simply sat down on the forest floor and refused to move.

"I'm sorry," Courtney said as she knelt beside the child. "She's exhausted and scared and probably hungry."

That pretty much summed up Ronin's own feelings, and probably Courtney's, too. He couldn't blame a three-year-old for not knowing how to cope.

"Let's find a place to spend the night," he said. "We could all use a rest."

They found a place to camp in a bowl-shaped clearing left by a giant uprooted fir, the decaying trunk of which rose up like a wall on one side of the leaf-carpeted space. Ronin cut fir boughs and Courtney spread them on the ground, then lay the blanket over them. Ashlyn lay on this bed and watched them until she fell asleep. He cut more boughs and together they built a lean-to perpendicular to the tree trunk, then he set about building a campfire.

"Is that safe?" Courtney asked. "Won't that lead him right to us?" She didn't say "Trey".

"The breeze is blowing the smoke away from the direction we came," Ronin said. "And he's not going to be able to travel in the dark any better than we can." Already the light had faded to the point where the surrounding forest was a collection of dark and darker shadows.

"He was in the army," she said. "Don't they train them for stuff like that?"

"We'll keep the fire small," he said, holding a lit

match to the tinder and watching it catch. "I think it will be okay."

She settled onto the blanket beside Ashlyn and looked down on the sleeping child. "My poor baby is exhausted," she said.

Courtney sounded exhausted, too. Ronin settled next to her. "Tell me what happened," he said. As a deputy, he wanted the details of the crime that had been committed against her.

As a man who cared about her, he wanted to give her the opportunity to share what she had experienced. He wanted her to trust him with that.

She closed her eyes and sighed, a long, weary breath that made him ache for her. "I was planning to leave him," she said. "I put my important papers in the lining of my purse, along with three little gold bars from a stash I found in his shed."

Ronin touched her arm. "Where did he get the gold bars?"

"I don't know. They were in an old backpack in the shed. He forgot to lock up one day and after he left I went in there and found them. I knew I'd need money after we left, so I took three."

"I think he stole them from Martin Kramer," Ronin said. "Kramer kept them in a strongbox in his mine. After he was arrested, his daughter reported them missing."

She leaned her head on his shoulder. "I thought Trey was a completely different man than he turned out to be. Why didn't I see that?"

Ronin put his arm around her and felt her relax

against him more. "He deliberately set out to deceive you," he said. "He fooled a lot of people."

"He told me if I tried to leave him, he'd take Ashlyn and I'd never see her again." She glanced at the sleeping child and lowered her voice. "He threatened to kill her, or…or to sell her." She choked on the last words and Ronin held her tighter.

The hatred he felt toward Trey Allerton was almost as overwhelming as the fierce desire to protect Courtney and Ashlyn. "We won't let him harm her," he said, struggling to quell the storm of emotion.

She nodded, and sat up a little straighter, though he still kept his arm around her. "That day we met, on the side of the road. I was trying to leave. I thought I'd get the Olsens to drive me into town, and the sheriff's department would help me get Ashlyn away from him before he realized what had happened. He took her with him so much because he knew I wouldn't leave her behind. I thought I could outsmart him, but I was wrong."

She fell silent and he waited, staring into the fire and trying not to think about all the ways he wanted to hurt Trey Allerton.

"I decided I would wait until one day when he left Ashlyn at home with me. He did that sometimes. I thought I could make it to the Olsens', or maybe I'd get one of the construction workers to help. I didn't really have a plan. I just wanted to be ready."

"You could have asked me for help," he said.

"Trey hates cops. I was afraid of what he would do to you or anyone who helped me. I even hesitated to involve the Olsens but I thought I could get to them and the sheriff before Trey found out, and that he would never have to know they helped me." She shook her head. "I couldn't risk him hurting you."

His chest tightened at her words. "I take it he found out what you were planning?"

"Yes. He stayed up after I went to bed last night and I guess he went through my things. He found the gold and the papers in my purse. He was so furious." A shudder went through her. "He dragged me and Ashlyn out of bed at four thirty this morning, had us get dressed, then drove us up to the trailhead. He carried Ashlyn and forced me to hike with them up to that... that underground room. When I wouldn't go inside, he hit me and threw me in, and shoved Ashlyn in after me and locked the door." Another shudder. "I thought he'd buried us alive and just...left us."

She began to sob, and he held her, his anger warring with compassion for all she had been through. "I'll find him," he said. "And I'll make sure he's punished."

After a while, her weeping subsided. He continued to hold her, feeling more alive than he had in a long time. He would do anything to protect this woman and her child. The knowledge awed him and made him stronger.

Ashlyn stirred and opened her eyes. "I'm hungry," she said.

Ronin retrieved his pack. "There're still some protein bars left." He dug until he found the bars, and handed them both to Courtney. "You and Ashlyn can share."

"What about you?" she asked.

"I had a big lunch." That seemed like a long time ago now, but it wouldn't hurt him to skip a meal, and Courtney and her daughter hadn't eaten in almost twenty-four hours.

Ashlyn crawled over and sat between them, munching on the protein bar. She leaned against her mother, but didn't seem to mind Ronin's presence on her other side. "I like the fire," she said after a while.

"It's nice," Courtney said.

Ronin leaned forward and added another stick to the small blaze. It gave off more light than heat, but was comforting. He wondered if he could capture the play of color amongst the coals in a photograph.

A light pressure on his thigh distracted him and he realized Ashlyn was patting him. When he looked down at her, she stared up at him, her blue eyes questioning. "Why did Trey lock us up in that place?" she asked.

Ronin looked across the top of her head to Courtney. How was he supposed to answer? What was appropriate for a three-year-old?

"Sometimes people we think are good turn out to be bad," Courtney said. "Trey is bad for locking us up like that, but we're not going to ever let him hurt us again."

"We're not," Ronin confirmed.

COURTNEY WANTED TO believe what she and Ronin had told Ashlyn, but she also knew that Trey wasn't going to let her get away from him without a fight. Over the past few months she had come to realize that Trey was obsessed with her and Ashlyn. It was as if he was convinced that they belonged with him—that they belonged *to* him.

Ashlyn yawned and lay across her mother's lap. Ronin opened the pack again and took out his spare clothes. "The two of you put these on," he said. "It will be colder tonight."

"You should take them," Courtney said.

"I'm fine."

She didn't believe him, any more than she had believed his lie about not being hungry. But she wasn't going to change his mind by arguing, so she took the clothes. "Thank you," she said.

She dressed Ashlyn in the sweatshirt and took the jacket and pants for herself. Then she wrapped the child in the blanket and settled her nearer the fire, on the end of the piled-up branches.

Without the buffer of the child between them, she was acutely aware of Ronin—of the warmth radiating from his body, of his muscular thigh brushing hers as he leaned forward to move another log onto the fire. She watched him out of the corner of her eye, mesmerized by the dark shadow across his jaw where he needed a shave, and the strong jut of his nose. Everything about him spoke of strength and a confidence she envied.

He glanced over and caught her staring. She looked away, but tried to cover the awkwardness of the moment. "I've told you all about my day," she said. "How was yours? What were you doing at those ruins?"

"I was photographing those buildings." He extended his arms out in front of him and rolled his head, stretching. "My gallery showing was today and I wanted to unwind after that."

"How was the show?" She angled toward him. "Did a lot of people come?"

He nodded. "More than I expected. Friends and some of the people I work with, but others, too. I even sold a few pieces, and the gallery owner is sure I'll sell more."

"That's wonderful. I wish I could have been there."

His gaze met hers and heat pooled in her middle, radiating outward. "I wish you could have been there, too," he said, his voice a little rough.

Her mouth was dry, and she struggled to swallow. His gaze remained fixed on her, flames reflected in the dark pools of his pupils. He wasn't physically touching her, yet she felt him so keenly, intimate feelings that had her aroused and on edge. The darkness was like a cloak around them, shutting out everything and everyone. It was exciting and thrilling, but she didn't trust her emotions right now.

She had done so many things she regretted. She didn't want to make another mistake. "How did you become interested in photography?" she asked.

"I found a camera in the hall closet when I was ten and started tinkering with it," he said. "I learned how to use it and started to carry it everywhere. I ended up spending every penny I could get my hands on film." He shrugged. "I was kind of a loner as a kid, and photography was something I could do by myself."

"Why were you a loner?" she asked, intrigued. She had been one of the popular girls, part of a big social group. Only since Mike's deployment had she learned to enjoy her own company.

He rested his wrists on his upraised knees and stared into the fire. For a long time he didn't say anything, and she wondered if she had offended him. "Was that a rude question?" she asked. "I'm sorry."

"Don't be sorry. And it wasn't a rude question, I'm just trying to decide what to say."

"You don't have to say anything." She certainly had enough things in her own life that she'd prefer to keep private.

"No, I want to tell you." He leaned forward to push a branch further into the fire. "My dad had a terrible temper," he said. "He hit my mom, and sometimes my brother and me. We spent all our time trying to avoid making him angry, but we didn't always succeed." He glanced at her, as if gauging her reaction. "When I was a kid, I never understood why she didn't just leave him. As I got older, and especially after I went to work in law enforcement, I realized the reality of the situation isn't always so cut-and-dried."

His words were like physical blows, battering her defenses. She began to weep, shame and grief overwhelming her.

Ronin put his arm around her and pulled her close. "Hey! I didn't mean to make you cry."

"I've made so many mistakes," she sobbed. "I should never have let Trey talk me into coming here with him. I should never have given him money. But he could be so sweet and charming, and I was so lonely..."

"People like Trey know how to manipulate others,"

Ronin said. "You did the best you could—I believe that."

"I wish I could." She sniffed and wiped at her eyes. "I'm so afraid I've damaged Ashlyn for life, exposing her to…to all of this." She looked around her at the dark woods.

"Children are resilient," Ronin said. "I went through some dark times and I turned out okay. No matter what happened with my dad, I knew my mother loved me. Ashlyn knows you love her. And the worst is past you now."

"Do you think so? Trey is still looking for us and I know he won't give up easily. I told myself I could walk away and he'd let me go, but after he locked us in that building…" Those nightmare hours in that dark, cold space had showed her the depths of Trey's determination to keep her under his control.

"I won't let him get to you or Ashlyn." Ronin's voice was hard, and his grip on her tightened. "And I'll make sure he pays for what he's already done to you."

She lifted her gaze to his again, drawing strength from the reassurance he offered, letting the warmth he kindled in her burn away her weakness and fear.

She pressed one hand to his chest and felt the hard beating of his heart, then caressed his shoulder and slipped her hand around to the back of his head, the thick silk of his hair against her fingers.

She coaxed his mouth closer to hers, then kissed him, all the passion and need she had kept locked away for so long rising into that kiss.

He was so gentle with her, yet not tentative, the

firm caress of his lips coaxing life into nerves she had thought too deadened by pain and absence to ever feel anything again. She arched against him, pressing her breasts against his chest, reveling in the sensation of the softly feminine against the hard masculine. She crooned with delight, and angled her head to deepen the kiss, inviting his tongue to dance with hers, the heat and taste of him leaving her breathless and wanting more.

His hands grasped her waist, then slid up to cup her breasts, and the knowledge that he wanted her as much as she wanted him made her smile. She touched the top button of his wool shirt, but before she could unfasten in, Ashlyn whimpered and she froze—brought back to herself and her responsibilities.

She drew away and smoothed her clothes, not looking at him, focusing instead on Ashlyn, who was moving fitfully, as if in the throes of a bad dream.

She moved to kneel beside the little girl, and put a hand on her arm. "It's okay," she murmured. "Mommy's here. Everything is okay."

Ronin stood and walked away. Was he angry, or merely frustrated? But he returned seconds later with an armload of wood. "I'll build up the fire," he said. "It will make her more comfortable." Then he smiled, a genuine look filled with warmth, not one of Trey's overly charming smiles that lately left her chilled and uneasy.

"We should get some rest," he said. "We'll want to leave at first light." He squatted beside the fire and began to add logs to the blaze. "You and Ashlyn take the blanket. I'm going to stay up and keep watch."

"You have to sleep, too," she said.

"I'll doze a little." He stood and they faced each other across the fire.

"I really like you," she blurted. "But my life is so complicated right now."

"I know." He held out both hands. "No expectations," he said. "And no pressure. I'm here if you need me."

She nodded. "Thank you."

She lay down beside her daughter and closed her eyes, but for a long time she didn't sleep. She listened to the crackle of the fire and to Ronin moving around the camp and tried not to worry about all the uncertainties ahead.

When she woke again, she was stiff and cold. Gray light filtered through the trees, reducing the scene to a charcoal drawing. She sat up and stretched, wincing as pain lanced through her sore muscles. The fire had gone out and Ronin lay on the other side of it, head cradled on his arm, eyes closed.

Trying to move as soundlessly as possible, Courtney stood. She winced as a branch crackled beneath her, then came more awake as the sense of something wrong swept over her. She looked around, fighting panic. "Ashlyn?" she called, then louder, "Ashlyn!"

Ronin sat up. "What is it?" he asked. "What's wrong?"

"Ashlyn's gone," she said, shaking now. "My baby's gone."

Chapter Thirteen

Courtney's anguished cry jolted Ronin awake. He scanned the area around the camp, but Ashlyn was nowhere in sight. "When did you see her last?" he asked.

"She was here when I fell asleep. I never heard her leave." She turned, scanning the woods around her. "Ashlyn!" she shouted again.

"She was here when I lay down, too," Ronin said. "That was only a couple of hours ago." He had told himself he wouldn't sleep deeply on the hard ground—he would only snatch a little rest before they had to set out again on what would likely be a miles-long hike over rough terrain. He was certain no one could have entered camp without him knowing.

He looked down at his sweatshirt, which lay on the blanket. Ashlyn had been wearing it when Courtney put her to bed for the night. "Maybe she went into the woods to use the bathroom," he said. He picked up the shirt and examined it, but it was dry and clean, with no sign of damage.

"She probably took that off during the night," Courtney said. "She gets hot in her sleep." She studied the ground, but the dry soil showed no sign of which direction the child might have wandered. "Ashlyn!" Courtney cried again, a note of panic in her voice. "Ashlyn, answer me."

"She can't have wandered far," Ronin said, though he had heard stories of lost children who walked for miles. "Ashlyn!" he shouted.

His voice echoed back to him and he strained his ears for a reply, but none came.

"We have to look for her." Courtney picked up the blanket and wrapped it around herself. Ronin stuffed the sweatshirt into his pack, then snagged Courtney's arm as she started to leave the depression where they had camped.

"We need to stay together," he said. "We can't risk one of us getting lost."

She nodded, and pulled the blanket more tightly around herself. "But please, we need to hurry."

Ronin looked around them. To the north, the ground rose steeply, to a wall of rock that rose up a hundred yards or more. He doubted Ashlyn would have tried to climb up there. To the south the ground fell away in an uneven morass of fallen trees and scattered boulders. The easiest way lay east, the way they had come, and west. "Do you think Ashlyn would be more likely to go back the way we came, or to head east?" he asked.

Courtney bit her lip. "Maybe—the way we had come? At least, that might have looked familiar to her. If she did go to use the bathroom and got turned around trying to find her way back to camp…" She stared over her shoulder, into the stretch of woods they had traversed yesterday. Surely that was all that had happened—Ashlyn had just wandered off for a moment. It couldn't be something worse.

"Let's go." Ronin touched her shoulder and she nodded and followed him out of the little clearing and into the denser trees. "Ashlyn!" he shouted.

"Ashlyn!" Courtney echoed.

He scanned the woods, hoping for some movement, or a flash of Ashlyn's blond hair or the blue of her shirt. The area was eerily silent—had their shouts frightened away the birds and other small animals who usually populated the forest with sound.

"Ashlyn!" Courtney's voice was ragged with tears.

"Mommy!"

They froze, Courtney clutching Ronin's arm. The fear in the child's high-pitched voice sent a jolt of adrenaline through him.

"Ashlyn!" Courtney's fingers dug into the fabric of his shirt. "Ashlyn, where are you?"

"Up here!" A second voice, masculine and taunting, had Ronin reaching for his pistol.

"Trey!" Courtney pointed to a ridge to the north. A hundred yards above them, out of reach of Ronin's pistol, Trey Allerton stood, a sobbing Ashlyn clasped to his chest.

"I told you if you left, you'd never see her again!" Trey shouted.

"No!" Courtney shouted. "Don't hurt her. I'll come back, I promise. Please don't hurt her."

"It's too late," Trey shouted. Then he turned and

was gone, disappearing into the shadows of the trees and rocks.

Ronin holstered his weapon and started running up the slope. Courtney followed, but within only a few yards the incline was nearly vertical. They had to scramble on hands and knees across loose rock that shifted with almost every footfall, and detour around gnarled trees and tangles of dense shrubbery. It was impossible to gain much speed and by the time they reached the ledge where Trey had taunted them a quarter of an hour had passed. Ronin stood bent over, hands on his knees, trying to catch his breath.

Courtney was on her knees beside him, gasping and sobbing. "How did he get her?" she asked.

"I think he either waited until she left camp to use the bathroom, or he lured her away from camp, perhaps with food or a treat," Ronin said. He straightened and looked around them. The ground leveled out here, and a faint path led through the trees away from the ledge. The soft dawn light flooded the spaces between the trees and the air smelled green and fertile. Dozens of birds flitted overhead, their various songs mingling with the rustle of the breeze through leaves in a restless chorus.

He offered Courtney his hand. "Let's see where this path goes," he said.

She clasped his hand and he pulled her up, then they hurried along the path. He drew his pistol and moved cautiously, aware of the possibility of a trap.

But the path opened out onto the shoulder of a dirt

forest service road, faint tracks in the dirt indicating where someone had pulled over here recently.

"They're gone," Courtney said. "How are we going to find them now?"

Ronin checked the angle of the sun and reviewed his knowledge of the area. "I think this is the forest service road that eventually becomes County Road 361," he said. "If we head south, we should come to the county road in a few miles. We can reach the Olsens and ask them to drive us to town, or call for help." He had no idea if the Olsens had a phone, but maybe they did.

"We can't leave," Courtney said. "Not until we know what happened to Ashlyn."

"The sheriff's department can help us look for her," Ronin said. "They can bring in search dogs and drones and aircraft. And they can issue an alert for Trey Allerton, making it more difficult for him to travel."

Hope sparked in her eyes and she grabbed his hand. "Do you really think we can find her?"

He wanted to reassure her that they would find Trey and that no harm would come to Ashlyn. But too many aspects of this situation were out of his control. He had no idea what Trey intended or where he had gone from here. Was he working alone, or did he have someone helping him? Had he made a plan in advance, or was he acting on impulse? "We'll do everything in our power to find her," he said. "The sooner we act, and the more people we have searching, the better our chances for success."

"Then let's hurry," she said, and started down the road, so that he had to jog to catch up with her. All the while, the image of Ashlyn, crying in Trey Allerton's arm, filled his mind. He was exhausted and hungry and worried about Courtney, but the image of that little girl would keep him going. He would do anything to bring her home safely to her mother.

FEAR WAS A DRUG that paralyzed Courtney. It numbed her to everything around her and prevented most of what others said to her from sinking in.

She had little memory of their frantic journey down the forest service road to the county road, though the trip felt as if it took hours. Her senses were frayed to the point of breaking with the strain of constantly searching for Trey and Ashlyn, and fighting not to imagine what might happen to the little girl. She all but collapsed when they finally reached the yurt where her neighbors, Robby and Becca Olsen, greeted them with concern, and then alarm.

She recalled sitting in the back seat of a small car, pressed against Ronin, who kept his arm around her as if he feared she might drift away, while they raced to town. At the sheriff's department, Ronin had done most of the talking. The sheriff and others had listened, faces grave. They had asked her a few questions—what was Ashlyn wearing? Did Courtney have any idea where Trey might go? She had tried to answer, but it was hard to get the words past the panic that threatened to overwhelm her. It took all her strength just to hold it back.

An older woman named Adelaide brought her coffee she couldn't drink, and Ronin brought her food she couldn't eat. She forced herself to sip water and tried to breathe deeply. She needed to keep it together for Ashlyn's sake. When they found her little girl, Ashlyn would need her mother. Ronin put her in a little room with a table and chair and asked her to wait while he worked and she'd nodded and sat, and stared at the wall, cold all over.

She couldn't even cry any more. It was as if the tears were frozen inside her. The only thing that wasn't immobilized and silenced by her terror was the voice in her head which sneered that she never should have left Trey.

If she had stayed with him, this never would have happened. Ashlyn would be safe.

She didn't know how long she sat in the little room by herself before Ronin returned. He sat at the table beside her and took her hand in his. He had big hands, warm with long, gentle fingers. "How are you doing?" he asked.

"Have you learned anything?" she asked. "Do you know where she is?"

"Not yet, but we've sent an Amber Alert with Trey and Ashlyn's descriptions and photos to every law enforcement agency in Colorado, Utah, New Mexico, Wyoming and Nebraska," he said. "We've sent a tracking dog and handler back to our campsite and we've got an alert at every airport, train and bus station, and border crossing. If he tries to take Ashlyn anywhere, someone will see him."

"I should go home," she said. She sat up straighter, energized by the thought. "Trey might go back there. If he finds me there, maybe that will satisfy him and everything will be all right."

Ronin's expression was troubled. Hurt. "You don't

want to go back to Trey. Not after the way he treated you. The way he treated Ashlyn."

"I want my daughter to be safe," she said, her voice breaking. "If that's what it takes to keep her safe..."

"She'll never be safe with Trey," Ronin said. "The man belongs behind bars."

She nodded. Everything he said was true, but none of it mattered as long as Ashlyn was in danger. "I should go home," she said again.

Ronin looked down at their clasped hands. "I'm sorry, but you can't do that," he said. "The trailer—it's a wreck. We sent a team out there right away, to search for anything that might indicate where Trey had gone, and it's been trashed."

"Trey wrecked it?" She frowned. "That's not like him. He must be so furious." She swallowed hard. What if he took his anger out on Ashlyn?

"I can take you to a safe house," Ronin said. "In Junction."

"No. That's too far away." She pulled her hand from his grasp. "I need to be here, close. Isn't there somewhere I can stay here?"

He nodded. "Yes." He stood, and waited for her to stand also.

"Where are we going?" she asked.

"I'm taking you to my place. I know you'll be safe there."

THE HOUSE RONIN rented on a side street in Eagle Mountain had once been a miner's cabin. The wooden bungalow–style dwelling was painted sage green with white trim and had a small front porch flanked by wooden columns. The house had one bedroom, one bathroom, a den, a dining room he used as an office, and a compact kitchen with a breakfast nook, and a single car garage. Though showing its age in places, the house featured burnished cherry floors and stained glass transoms in most of the windows, plus mature fir trees that shaded the home from the summer heat.

"You can have the bedroom," Ronin said as he led Courtney into the house. "The sofa makes into a bed, so I'll be fine there." He showed her the bathroom and the kitchen, then realized she had no luggage. "You probably want a change of clothes. I'll ask Adelaide to pick you up a few things."

"I'll call Lauren," she said. "I need to tell her what's going on. And she probably has some clothes I can borrow." She looked down at her dirty jeans and sneakers. "Did Trey destroy everything? Even my clothes?"

"There are probably some things you can retrieve later," he said. "I didn't see it, but apparently everything was pulled out of drawers and thrown around."

She frowned. "I don't understand why Trey would do that. Do you think it was someone else—looking for something?"

"We're considering that. Can you think of anyone who might be looking for something Trey might have?"

"You said the gold bars belonged to Martin Kramer. But he's still in jail, isn't he?"

"I'll check on that. Meanwhile, you could help by making a list of everyone you're aware of Trey doing business with in the last year or so. We'll want to contact them and see if Trey has been in touch. It's possible he has someone helping him to hide out right now."

"It will be a short list," she said. "Trey didn't really include me in his business dealings. It was one of the things we fought about. He wanted my money to build the camp, but he didn't want to include me in the planning and decision-making." She put a hand to her mouth. "What are we going to do about the children who are expecting to come to the camp in a couple of weeks? I think Trey may have collected money from some of their parents or sponsors."

"You can contact them later. Try not to worry about that now."

They were standing in the kitchen, so he went to the refrigerator and opened it. "Help yourself to anything you want to eat. There's coffee and tea in the cabinet, and crackers and cereal and stuff. If there's anything in particular you want, just text me and I'll stop by the store."

"I couldn't eat." She rubbed her stomach.

"Try," he said. "You want to keep your strength up. Ashlyn is going to need you."

She nodded. "I remembered something Trey said once, when he was threatening to hurt her if I left him. He said…" She swallowed, all color drained from her face. Ronin put his arm around her and she leaned against him. "He said he could sell her to people who would take her away and…and do horrible things to her." She buried her face against him, choking back sobs.

Ronin held her, fighting an anger that blurred his vision.

After a while, Courtney's sobs subsided and she pushed away from him. "I'm sorry," she said. "I don't mean to keep falling apart."

"You don't need to apologize," he said. "Will you call Lauren now? Maybe she can come stay with you. I hate to leave you here alone."

"I'll be okay. I'm used to being by myself. But I promise I will call Lauren, after you leave." She tried to smile, and almost succeeded. "I'll probably start crying again when I talk to her and you've seen enough of my tears."

His phone buzzed and he checked the screen to find a message from the sheriff about a meeting in half an hour. "I need to go," he said. "Call if you need anything. And don't let anyone in but me or Lauren or an officer you know. We're going to have someone patrolling in the area."

"I'll be careful. And you'll let me know the minute you hear anything?"

"I promise." He stepped forward, and started to kiss her, but held back. She was so vulnerable now. He wanted to comfort her however he could, but he didn't want to take advantage.

She took the initiative and moved forward to kiss him. "Thank you," she whispered. "For everything."

His mind was a jumble of thoughts as he drove back to the sheriff's department. How had Trey tracked them through the woods without Ronin realizing they were being followed? Why had he targeted Ashlyn, and not

Courtney, or even Ronin? And the biggest question of all—where was he now and how were they going to find him?

Adelaide greeted him as soon as he entered the building. "Detective Fletcher is here to see you," she said. "He wouldn't tell me what it's about."

Ronin followed her back out to the reception area, where Jim Fletcher waited. "I heard about Trey Allerton and that little girl," he said. "I just wanted to offer any help you might need."

"Thanks," Ronin said. "We don't have much to go on just yet."

"So you don't know where Allerton might be?" Fletcher asked. "What he might be up to?"

"Not yet."

"Why did he take the girl?" Fletcher asked. "And who is she?"

"She's the daughter of the woman Allerton was living with. He may have taken her as revenge for the woman leaving him."

"I guess you've searched his trailer?"

"Yes, we had a team out there to search it."

"Find anything?"

"Allerton—or someone else—had trashed the place," Ronin said. "We didn't find anything to indicate where he might have gone."

Fletcher nodded. "But did you find anything to indicate Allerton had been involved in criminal activity?"

Even though Fletcher was a cop, the question struck Ronin as odd. "What kind of activity?"

Fletcher shrugged. "I was just wondering if Allerton was linked to my case after all."

"I haven't seen the full report," Ronin said. "But I haven't heard anything."

"Let me know if you do," Fletcher said. "Just as a professional courtesy." He clapped a hand on Ronin's shoulder. "I'll let you get back to work. Keep me posted if there's anything I can do to help."

Ronin stared after the detective as he walked away. The whole exchange had struck him as odd. Sergeant Gage Walker passed Fletcher in the hallway. "Have you talked to Dwight yet?" Gage asked when he saw Ronin.

"No, why?" Ronin hadn't seen Deputy Dwight Prentice since he and Courtney had reported to the sheriff's department that afternoon.

"He was part of the team we sent to search Trey Allerton's trailer. Come in here a minute." Gage led the way into his office, a cramped space next to the squad room. He removed a stack of binders from a chair in front of his desk. "Have a seat. You look exhausted."

Ronin sat. Other than a couple of fitful hours on the cold ground early this morning, he hadn't slept in thirty-six hours. "Did Dwight find something at Allerton's place?" he asked.

"He found something, though I don't know if it will help us find Allerton." Gage settled into the chair behind his desk and took out his phone. "He sent over some pictures." He turned the screen to face Ronin, who leaned forward to study the photographs of a trunk filled with clothing, including a couple of wigs.

"Are those costumes?" he asked.

"They are." Gage flipped the phone around so that he could look at it again. "They fit the description of outfits worn by Bart Smith, both here and in Delta."

Ronin sagged back in the chair. "So Trey Allerton is Bart Smith?"

"It's him or he knows him," Gage said. "I'm betting the former. We'll try to have the costumes tested for DNA, see if Allerton wore them." He pocketed the phone again. "We found some other items in the trunk with the costumes. A lot of photographs of Courtney—not just recent pictures, but what looks like her high school graduation picture, and wedding photos. There were some candid shots, too, taken when it was obvious she didn't know she was being photographed—pictures of her sleeping, and a couple when she was in the shower. I got the impression Allerton was obsessed with her, and not in a good way."

"No, not in a good way." Ronin pushed down another wave of anger. "I think that's why he took Ashlyn. He wanted to hurt Courtney in the worst way possible."

"We're going to need to talk to Courtney about all of this," Gage said.

Ronin wanted to protest that Courtney was already on the edge of a breakdown because of her missing daughter, but instead he said, "I don't know how much she'll be able to tell you. She said Trey was very secretive about his activities."

"We had ruled out Allerton as Bart Smith because Courtney provided him with solid alibis that made it impossible for him to have been where Bart Smith was known to be," Gage said. "But these costumes make me question those alibis. You know her better than the rest of us—do you think she would have lied for him?"

Ronin's stomach clenched. "I think she would do anything to protect her daughter," he said after a moment. "If Allerton threatened to hurt Ashlyn if she didn't do what he wanted…" He sighed. "She might have lied."

"Travis said you took her to your place," Gage said.

"Yes."

"Bring her back here. I want to get this out of the way as soon as possible."

"Yes, sir." He stood. As a man who cared about Courtney, it was the last thing he wanted to do. As a law enforcement officer, he had a duty to look past his personal feelings in the interest of justice.

Chapter Fourteen

Lauren came to Ronin's house soon after Courtney called. "I've been so worried about you," she said, and pulled Courtney into a long embrace. She stared into the younger woman's face. "How are you doing?"

"I'm a wreck." Courtney led the way into the living room and sank onto the sofa.

"Of course you are." Lauren slipped a tote bag from her shoulder and began pulling items from it. "I brought some things that should help you a little bit. Comfortable, cute clothes—" She set out a pair of leggings, cozy socks, a soft knit tunic and a tank top. "A little makeup. Chocolates and good coffee." She held up each item as she added it to the growing pile on the end of the sofa. "Cookies. Chicken soup—it's not homemade, but as good as." She folded the empty tote. "And I can offer a prescription to help you sleep or something for anxiety if you think you need it. It's not unwarranted, considering the circumstances."

Courtney stared at the pile of gifts, stunned. "I'm not sick," she said.

"Of course you are. You're sick at heart over Ashlyn."

Lauren sat beside her. "I talked to Shane and everyone at the sheriff's department is upset over this. They are going to work their tails off to find Ashlyn."

"I feel so helpless," Courtney said. "I want to be doing something to help, but there isn't anything."

Lauren squeezed her hand. "I know, honey, but every minute you are sitting here worrying, just know you've got a whole bunch of men and women doing everything in their power to help. Ashlyn is their number one priority right now."

Courtney blotted tears with her fingers. "I'm so sick of crying!"

"Why don't you take a shower and get into some fresh clothes," Lauren said. "I'll heat some soup and make fresh coffee. All that will help you feel a little better."

Courtney didn't have much faith in this prescription, but standing in the shower, letting hot water run over her and steam rise up around her did feel surprisingly good. By the time she had dried her hair and slipped into the fresh clothing Lauren had brought, she felt stronger and less frayed. She even put on a little makeup, grateful to be able to look at herself in the mirror and not see someone who looked as washed out as she felt.

She found Lauren in the kitchen, setting the table for their meal. "There's soup and bread and for dessert we'll have coffee and cookies," Lauren said, and directed Courtney to a chair across from her.

The soup tasted so good, and its savory warmth was comforting. When the bowls were empty, Lauren poured coffee and set a plate of warm cookies between them. "Tell me everything," Lauren said. "Partly because I'm nosy and partly because I think talking about it will help you."

Slowly, haltingly at first then with more feeling, Courtney told about preparing to leave Trey, him locking her and Ashlyn in that underground room and Ronin finding them, being shot at, escaping through the woods, and waking to find Ashlyn missing, their search, then being taunted by Trey. Most of it she had already told Ronin, and some of it she had repeated at the sheriff's department, but recounting the whole story to Lauren felt different—more sharing than unburdening. Maybe it was because Lauren was Ashlyn's aunt and godmother, the one other person who had been a part of Ashlyn's life since the hour of her birth, who loved her almost as much as Courtney.

"That man is evil," Lauren said when Courtney had finally revealed everything.

"You never liked him," Courtney said. "Why couldn't I see him the way you did?"

Lauren took a bite of her cookie and chewed, looking thoughtful. "I think he was different with you than he was with me," she said after a moment. "And you were vulnerable, alone and still grieving for Mike. Trey used that against you. He told you all those stories about him and Mike, making you believe Mike would have wanted you to be with him."

"Now I think all those things he said were lies." She couldn't say why it had taken her so long to realize this. All the clues had been there, but it was as if

Trey had hypnotized her, so that she only saw things from his point of view. Now it was as if she had woken from a stupor, and could see clearly again after so many months of limited vision. "I mean, he must have known Mike," she said. "He had a picture of me that I'd given to Mike, and he knew so much about me. But I don't think they were friends. Mike never mentioned him. Not once." She shook her head. "I can't believe I was so stupid."

"Stop it." Lauren's voice was stern. "You're not stupid. You like to think the best of people and that's not a bad thing. Maybe you were naive, but that's not a crime, or a moral failing."

Courtney nodded. She wanted to believe Lauren's words were true, but she wasn't there yet. "Thanks for coming over tonight," she said. "Having you here is a big help."

Lauren got up and refilled their coffee. "This is a cozy little place Ronin has." She studied a trio of framed photos on the wall by the table—close-ups of wildflowers. "Shane and I went to his gallery showing yesterday."

"He said there was a good turnout."

"There were a lot of people there. We even bought one of his photos. He's an amazing talent." She smiled. "And good-looking, too."

Courtney's cheeks heated. "He is."

"He asked about you at the showing. I got the impression he really likes you."

"I really like him." The words burst from her, a guilty secret she couldn't hold back any longer. "But everything is so strange right now." Were her feelings for Ronin real, or just another attempt to latch on to the closest man who paid attention to her when she was dealing with difficult emotions?

"You don't need to rush into anything," Lauren said. "But it's nice knowing there's a good, decent man who's noticed how much you have to offer."

"I don't have anything to offer right now. I'm a wreck."

They both fell silent at the sound of a vehicle pulling up outside. Lauren moved to the window and peered out. "It's Ronin."

Relief flooded Courtney, followed closely by agitation. What if he had news? What if the news wasn't good?

The women waited in the kitchen as Ronin opened the front door. "We're in the kitchen," Lauren called.

Courtney's first thought was that he looked so exhausted, his whole body sagging with the burden of the past couple of days. "Hello, Lauren," he said, then turned to Courtney. "No news yet," he said, answering her unspoken question. "But we need you to come down to the station. We found some things of Trey's at the trailer and we need to ask you about them."

"Do you want me to come with you?" Lauren asked.

"That's okay. I'll be fine with Ronin."

She stood and gathered her purse, then followed him to the door. Lauren hugged her goodbye while Ronin locked the door behind them, then he led the way to his patrol SUV. He waited until they were inside and

Lauren had driven away before he spoke again. "Do you have a lawyer?" he asked.

"I...only the one who handles my trust."

"Maybe you should call him, and ask him to recommend someone. A criminal lawyer."

She couldn't breathe, and her vision blurred. "Why? What's happened? Am I being accused of some crime?"

Ronin made a sound like a stifled groan. "Some of the things the team found in Trey's shed call into question some of the statements you've made to the sheriff's department before," he said. "It would be a good idea if you had some legal representation. I can't really say any more."

She sank back and closed her eyes. She had known this was coming, hadn't she? Trey had warned her, even.

"I'm sorry," Ronin said.

She opened her eyes and looked at him. "Don't be." She took out her phone. "I'll call my lawyer. Thank you for suggesting it." If she was in trouble, it wasn't because of anything Ronin had done. She had only herself to blame.

RONIN WOULD HAVE predicted they would need to postpone questioning Courtney until the next day, but her attorney in Denver must have had some influence, because by the time he and Courtney arrived at the sheriff's department she had spoken not only to her lawyer, but to a criminal attorney he recommended, who agreed to come right away.

While they waited for the attorney to arrive, Ronin

returned to his desk and tried to focus on anything but the hurting woman in the interview room. He dialed Jim Fletcher's cell phone, but the call went straight to voice mail. "Hey, Jim, it's Ronin Doyle. Give me a call when you get this." He ended the call, then stared at the phone in his hand. Delta PD had approached Rayford County about helping them to find Bart Smith, so he felt an obligation to let them know he was pretty sure they had found the elusive Smith. If he left it until morning, word might very well have spread, particularly if anyone in the media heard about this.

He punched in the main number for the Delta Police Department. If Fletcher wasn't in, he'd ask to talk to someone else connected with the case. He identified himself to the man who answered the phone, then asked for Jim Fletcher.

"You say you're with the Rayford County Sheriff's Department?" the man asked.

"Yes. Deputy Ronin Doyle. I've been working with Fletcher on a case."

"Let me put you through to Detective Fletcher's supervisor."

Ronin waited through half a chorus of an '80s pop song then a gravelly voice asked, "What do you need to speak to Fletcher about, Deputy?"

"He came to us asking for help in finding Bart Smith and we have a new lead," Ronin said.

"When was this?" the man asked.

"Excuse me, who is this?" Ronin asked.

"This is Assistant Police Chief Will Jory. When did Fletcher ask Rayford County for assistance?"

"It's been about two weeks," Ronin said. "Why?"

"Because Detective Fletcher has been on administrative leave for two weeks," Jory said.

"Why is he on leave?"

"He was put on leave pending an investigation. Who is Bart Smith?"

Ronin wondered if the lack of sleep was getting to him. "Detective Fletcher said you were looking for a man named Smith in connection with a ring of teenage drug dealers. Smith is the man who recruited them."

"We are working a drug case involving underage dealers," Jory said. "This is the first time I've heard of anyone named Smith."

"Are you saying Fletcher lied to us?"

"I'm saying I wouldn't trust anything Fletcher has to say," Jory said. "And if he contacts you again, you can refer him to me."

Ronin hung up the phone, feeling numb. Then he forced himself to stand and seek out the sheriff. "Delta P.D. tells me they've never heard of Bart Smith, and that Jim Fletcher has been on administrative leave—pending an investigation—for the past week."

Travis's eyes narrowed. "That doesn't sound good."

"No, it doesn't," Ronin said. "At the gallery yesterday, Fletcher didn't say anything about being on leave."

"It's not the kind of thing a lot of people would volunteer," Travis said.

"A couple of days before that, I saw him in town, talking to someone in an alley near the gallery. I couldn't see who he was talking to, but shortly after that Ashlyn Baker came out of the same alley. I went after her, but she had disappeared. The alley was empty. Yesterday, Fletcher made a point of telling me he had been talking to a parent who was giving Susan Richards a hard time."

"Do you think he was lying?" Travis asked.

"I wonder if he was talking to Trey and didn't want me to know." What kind of game was Fletcher playing? His phone call earlier took on a more suspicious tone. Ronin had thought Fletcher was truly concerned about the welfare of a child. But now it seemed as if he had merely been pumping Ronin for more information about Trey Allerton. But why?

TANYA DESTIN WAS a trim woman in her fifties with striking silver hair and kind brown eyes. She greeted Courtney warmly and immediately established herself as her client's advocate. Ronin could see Courtney visibly relax in her presence.

The sheriff and Gage handled the questioning, while Ronin stood at the back of the room. He felt an obligation to be there, to witness whatever was about to happen.

Travis began by reciting all the particulars for the recording. Then Gage laid out pictures of the items found in the trunk—Bart Smith's costumes.

"Do you recognize these?" Travis asked.

"I've never seen these before," Courtney said.

"You've never seen Trey Allerton wearing them?" Gage asked.

She shook her head. "No. Never."

Gage referred to his notes. "On July 10 you were

interviewed by Deputy Landry and stated that you and Mr. Allerton had been together all day and had arrived home only shortly before the deputy questioned you. Do you recall that interview?"

She was very pale. "Yes," she whispered.

"Please speak up for the recording," Gage said.

"Yes, I remember talking to the deputy."

"Do you still stand by the statement you made to the deputy that day?" Gage asked.

"You don't have to answer that," Ms. Destin said.

"No," Courtney said, then a little louder, "No, I don't stand by that statement. I… I lied." She looked, not at the officers, but at her attorney. "Trey threatened to hurt Ashlyn if I didn't say what he told me to."

"And on July 14, you again told me that Trey had been with you all day," Gage said. "Was that statement true?"

"No. I…I lied then, too. Trey said I had to give him an alibi. He…he told me he hadn't done anything wrong, but that the sheriff's department didn't have a right to pry into his private business." At last she looked at Gage and Travis. "I'm sorry. I know it was wrong, but I was so afraid he would hurt Ashlyn. And…and I wanted to believe Trey was a good man, because if he wasn't, didn't that make me a bad person for choosing him?"

Ms. Destin put her hand on Courtney's arm. "You're not a bad person," she said.

"Do you know where Trey was on July 10?" Gage asked.

"No. I promise I would tell you if I knew. He was

away from the house and that's all I knew. He never told me where he was going or what he was doing and if I asked he became angry."

"Why didn't you tell us the truth before now?" Gage asked.

"Because I was afraid."

"Because he threatened your daughter?" Gage asked.

"Yes, but also because he said if I went to the sheriff, I'd be arrested for lying." She looked at the attorney again. "Is that going to happen?"

"Clearly my client was under great duress when she lied to the sheriff's deputies," Ms. Destin said. "She feared for the safety of her child, and I'm sure for her own safety, as well. Anyone can understand a mother's instinct to protect her child. And clearly, Trey Allerton's threats were no idle gestures, since he has, in fact, kidnapped my client's daughter."

"We merely want to establish the facts of the situation," Travis said.

"I'll tell you everything I know," Courtney said.

"Not unless you agree not to bring charges," Ms. Destin said.

"It's not our intention to charge Ms. Baker if she cooperates," Travis said.

Courtney's shoulders relaxed, and Ronin felt her relief from across the room. The rest of the session was spent going over every detail Courtney remembered from the dates in question, though it wasn't much. Clearly, Trey had been very secretive about his activities.

"We also found a white Toyota Rav4 in a shed on

the property," Gage said. "The vehicle is registered to you."

"Trey told me he'd sold it," she said. "He said we needed the money to pay bills and I signed the title over to him. It was only Friday that I found out he hadn't sold it after all. We argued about it. He told me the man he had sold it to asked him to keep the car for a few weeks so he could surprise his daughter on her birthday. I told Trey he needed to cancel the sale but he refused. I think... I think that argument is what made him look through my things, to see what else I knew. He found the gold bars and important papers I'd hidden in my purse and knew I was getting ready to leave him. That's when he took Ashlyn and me and locked us up."

"So you have no knowledge of Trey Allerton driving the car on July 7 or July 13 or July 19?" Gage said.

"No, I thought he'd sold the Rav4. When I found it in that shed I couldn't understand why he'd lied to me." Her voice broke. "I didn't realize how many lies he told me from the very beginning."

"My client is clearly distraught and exhausted," Ms. Destin said. "She's answered enough questions for today and has done nothing any other loving parent wouldn't have done."

Travis looked pained. "We may have more questions later, but now she's free to go." He addressed Courtney. "Thank you for your cooperation, Ms. Baker."

He and Gage left the room and Ronin followed, but he lingered outside the door, waiting for the opportunity to talk to Courtney alone. A few moments later,

Ms. Destin emerged from the room. "Deputy Doyle?" she asked.

"Yes."

"Courtney would like to speak to you."

So she had known he was there. He slipped into the room and she turned to face him, her fingers gripping the edge of the table. He moved to sit beside her and took her hand. "I know that was hard on you," he said. "But you did great."

She pressed her lips together and looked away. "I understand if you don't want me to come back to your place," she said. "You didn't know I was a liar."

"No!" He touched the side of her face, coaxing her to look at him again. "None of us is perfect," he said. "And I understand why you said what you did."

"But you're a law enforcement officer," she said. "Your job depends on the truth and those things I said…maybe they helped Trey get away with worse things. If I'd told the truth…"

"If you'd told the truth, he might have hurt you and Ashlyn."

"I'm so worried he's hurting her now." Her eyes filled with tears and she bowed her head again.

"Come on." He wrapped both his hands around hers. "You've had a horrible day. I'm exhausted and I know you are, too. Let's go back to my place and try to get some rest."

She nodded and walked with him down the hall and out the back way. They passed Gage and he nodded to them. "Good night."

Neither of them spoke on the drive to his house. "Do

you need anything?" he asked once they were inside. "Something to sleep in or a toothbrush?"

"Lauren brought me everything I need."

"Then let's try to get some sleep."

She retreated to the bedroom and he folded out the sofa and made up the bed, then stripped to his underwear and crawled under the blankets. Weariness dragged at his muscles and made it hard to keep his eyes open, though once he lay down and switched off the lights, sleep eluded him. His mind insisted on replaying the events of the last twenty-four hours and tormenting him with what he could have done differently. If only he had stayed awake at their camp instead of falling asleep. If only he had insisted Courtney and Ashlyn leave the parking area while he stayed to confront Trey. If only...

Movement in the room had him instantly alert. He rose up on one elbow to see Courtney's outline in the doorway. "I didn't mean to wake you," she said.

"I wasn't asleep." He sat up. "Is something wrong?"

"I was wondering if I could stay in here with you." She moved to stand beside the sofa bed. Through the light from the front window he could see she was wearing a simple cotton nightgown. "Just to sleep," she said. "I'm too nervous in that room by myself. I keep imagining Trey coming in the window to get me." She gave a ragged laugh. "I guess it's like being a kid and thinking there are monsters under the bed. I'm being silly, but—"

"It's okay. I'll feel a lot better having you here with me, too." Now that she had mentioned the possibility of Trey trying to get to her, his mind was alive with the possibilities. He slid over and folded back the covers. "Come on."

She crawled in and pulled the covers up to her chin. "Good night," she said, and rolled over with her back to him.

He fought the instinct to reach for her and hold her close. She had made it clear she didn't want intimacy, and he was aware they were both wearing very little. If he wasn't so exhausted the arrangement might have made sleep impossible, but though he was aware of the weight of her beside him on the mattress and the soft scent of her, he found himself relaxing, his breath slowing to match the rhythm of her own breathing. His mind stopped racing, and he gratefully gave himself up to sleep.

Courtney woke to gray light showing in the front windows of an unfamiliar room. As she came more fully awake, she became aware of Ronin beside her in bed, his body only inches away, so warm and solid. Moving carefully so as not to wake him, she turned on her side to face him and studied his face, the shadow of unshaven whiskers on his jaw, his lips slightly parted and full. One shoulder peeked out from the covers, broad and muscled.

Desire pierced her, the intensity of the feeling shocking her. She wanted this man, more than she had wanted anyone in years. A small voice in her head told her she should feel guilty for thinking such things when her daughter was missing, but that voice was soon drowned out by the elation of knowing that Trey hadn't killed everything human and alive within her.

She couldn't do anything to bring Ashlyn back to her right now. Knowing that was torture, but the idea that for a few brief moments she might be able to forget, to find a physical release from the mental agony, was a temptation she didn't want to resist.

Chapter Fifteen

Ronin stirred, and after a second's hesitation, Courtney rested her hand on his shoulder, a gentle caress that sent another thrill through her.

He opened his eyes, the irises almost black in the dusky light. "Good morning," he said, his voice rough.

"Good morning." She shifted, moving a fraction of an inch closer.

"How did you sleep?" he asked.

"Much better than I expected." She had no memory of dreams or of waking at all. "I think I was so exhausted my body just gave up." She smoothed her hand along the top of his shoulder. "I'm feeling better now."

He quirked an eyebrow, a sexy look that made her breath catch. He copied her movements and caressed her shoulder. "Are you, now?"

"Yes!" The single syllable was an urgent whisper.

He smoothed his hand along her arm, down to her waist, tracing the curve of her thigh. He caressed her bare skin and she bent her leg to brush against his own. He continued to explore, his touch turning her insides to hot caramel, every nerve alive with wanting.

Then he moved away, and cool air shocked her heated skin as he lifted the covers. "Give me a minute," he said. "I'll be right back."

She had a fleeting glimpse of his almost-nude body as he left the room. Her instinct was to lie back and try to catch her breath, but as a door closed somewhere down the hall, she realized he had retreated to the bathroom, and she realized she needed to do the same.

When the bathroom door opened, she was waiting in the hallway. "My turn," she said, and darted in before he could answer. Cuddling on first waking sounded romantic, but she welcomed the opportunity to brush her teeth, run a comb through her hair and relieve herself.

Feeling fresher, she hurried back to the living room. Already the room was lighter. "What time is it?" she asked, looking around for a clock.

"A little before six." He held out an arm and she went to him.

His kiss now was even better than the one they had shared before, warmer and bolder. They were both more sure of where this was going to lead, though she didn't want to rush. She slid her arms around him and curled her body against his, reveling in the heat and weight and strength of him. He was still wearing his underwear, but his erection pressed against her, leaving no doubt about how he felt.

She hooked her thumb under the elastic at his waist and tugged. He pressed his mouth to her neck and shifted to allow her to push his underwear all the way down. Then he was removing her underwear as well, and sliding his hand beneath her gown to caress her breasts. "That feels so wonderful," she said. His hands moved over her with a kind of reverence instead of the roughness she had grown accustomed to from Trey.

No. She wouldn't think of Trey. She cupped Ronin's buttocks and squeezed, bringing him closer to her, then she hooked her leg over his thigh, so that he was positioned over the center of her arousal. He slipped his hand down between them and began to stroke, until her head fell back and she was panting with need.

He rolled onto his back, pulling her on top of him, and pushed the nightgown up and over her shoulders. She stripped it the rest of the way off and sent it sailing, then she was straddling him, naked, her breasts cradled in his hands. "You're so soft," he said. Then his eyes met hers, and the tenderness there brought the sudden sting of tears. "Yet you're the strongest woman I know."

She buried her face against his shoulder, not wanting him to see the tears. How many men had told her she was beautiful? She had heard it all her life. But Ronin had told her she was strong. She had felt weak and helpless so often in her life—how could he know his words meant more to her than any praise for her physical attributes.

He kissed the side of her neck. "Everything okay?" he asked.

She raised her head, able to smile now. "It's better than okay." She kissed his lips, a brief hard pressure of her mouth to his. "I want you, Ronin Doyle." She ground against him. "I want you right now."

He reached back one hand under the pillow and pulled out a condom packet. At her surprised look, he laughed. "This is one reason I went into the bathroom earlier," he said.

He started to tear open the packet, but she took it from him. "Let me."

She took her time rolling on the condom, reveling in the feel of him, all heat and hardness, and yet aware of the power of the moment, him braced against the force of his own desire, her teasing him, just a little. When he finally pulled her hands away with an impatient gesture, he softened the move by kissing her fingers, sending a new jolt of lust through her as his tongue swept across her fingertips. "I want you now," he growled.

She pressed her hands to his chest and positioned herself over him, then thrilled to the sensation of him filling her, stretching her, caressing sensitive nerve endings, sensation sparking through her. They moved together slowly at first, finding a rhythm, eyes locked, not shying away from that level of connection.

He shaped his hands to her hips, guiding her movements, then left her to her own devices as he rose up to capture the tip of one breast in his mouth. He moved to the other breast, and she slid one hand between them to finger herself, letting the tension build, anticipating the release to come. Then he pushed her hand away and took over, hard thrusts and gentle fingers working in concert to bring her to the edge and over.

Her climax rippled through her in hot waves, leaving her gasping and elated. He groaned and thrust against her, finally allowing for his release.

They lay together for a long time before they moved

apart, reveling in the afterglow, until their bodies cooled and he eased her off of him and removed the condom. She nestled against him, more relaxed than she could remember being in years. "Clearly, my fantasies didn't do you justice," he said.

She smiled against him, but didn't bother lifting her head. "Are you saying you've been fantasizing about me?"

"Absolutely. From that first day we met on the side of the road."

She had to prop herself up to look at him then. "Seriously? I looked terrible that day!"

"I guess I saw past that." He brushed his knuckles across her cheek. "Didn't you notice how I couldn't stay away from you? I kept thinking of excuses to stop by, just so I could see you again. I was pathetic."

"I was always glad to see you." She lay down again, head cradled on his chest. "And you weren't pathetic. You've been wonderful."

They didn't say anything else after that, and might have fallen back to sleep. At some point, Ronin slipped out of the bed and went to take a shower. By the time he returned, she had dressed and gone into the kitchen and started coffee. She was trying hard to hold on to the afterglow of their lovemaking, but the coldness of her real world was freezing out all that wonderful warmth. Trey had had Ashlyn twenty-four hours now, a very long time for a three-year-old. She wanted to believe he wouldn't really hurt her, but he was fast proving that every idea she had had about him was wrong.

They were finishing breakfast when Ronin's cell

phone rang. Seated beside him at the table, she could hear the caller clearly. It was the sheriff, alert and to the point. "We found some maps in the glove box of Courtney's Rav4," he said. "We want her to take a look and tell us if the markings on them were made by her or by Trey."

"What are the maps of?" Ronin asked.

"They're of Rayford County. There are several locations circled in red."

Ronin's eyes met Courtney's. "We'll be right over," he said. He ended the call and stood and began clearing the table.

"I heard the sheriff," she said. "Do you think those markings mean something?" Her pulse beat out a wild rhythm. "Places Trey might be now?"

"I don't know," Ronin said. "But we'll definitely check them out. Maybe we'll be lucky."

Maybe we'll find Ashlyn today. In a few hours, even. The thought was too fragile to say out loud, but she nurtured the spark the thought kindled. That light was enough to push back the darkness a little further. Enough to help her through another day.

RONIN STUDIED THE maps laid out on a table in the conference room of the sheriff's department. First was a state road map—the kind available at tourist bureaus across the state. Next, a map of the county produced by a local real estate firm. In addition to detailing county and forest service roads, this map included hiking and ski trails as well as popular attractions, including many mine ruins. A number of these attractions were circled with a red pen.

Finally, arranged together at one side of the table, were a set of topo maps for the county, with detailed information on hiking trails, waterways, elevation changes and other topographical details. Ronin had a very similar set of maps in the glove compartment of his Jeep, which he used for navigation to places he wanted to photograph.

"The highway map looks like one I had," Courtney said. "But I've never seen the others before. I mean, I usually use my phone when I need directions to drive someplace."

"A lot of this backcountry doesn't have phone service," Ronin said. He indicated the topo maps. "Hikers, maybe hunters and people like that use these."

"What are all these markings on this map?" Courtney asked, pointing to the county map.

"We were hoping you could tell us," Gage said. "You're sure you've never seen these before? Maybe Trey was looking one of them over one evening at home?"

"I'm sorry, but I've never seen them." She studied the county map. "He's circled a bunch of old mines in the mountains."

"Including the place where you and Ashlyn were being held when I found you." Ronin pointed to the pick and shovel emblem above the name Sanford Mine.

"Are these all mines he has circled?" She moved in beside him to study the map more closely. "No, this one's an old ski hill, and this one just says Ghost Town."

"We'll have to check them all out," Gage said. "That could take a while."

"Do you think he's taken Ashlyn to one of these?" Courtney's face paled. "He could have her locked up in one of them." She pressed her fist to her mouth, the horror of the idea of her daughter locked up in some cold, dark prison in the wilderness showing clearly in her eyes.

Ronin put a hand on her shoulder. "If she's in one of these places, we'll find her," he said.

"There must be a dozen sites circled," Gage said.

"I've been to most of these," Ronin said. "I've got photographs that might help us." He put a finger over the ghost town. "There's nothing here but a couple of piles of rotting logs that used to be buildings. It's a five-mile hike over rough terrain to get there. I doubt Trey could hide anything there."

"Then why circle it?" Gage asked.

"Maybe these are all possibilities he intended to check out," Courtney said.

"I doubt he'd use the building above the Sanford Mine again," Ronin said. "He'd have to buy a new lock, but we should check it out."

"Where else might he go?" Gage asked. "What sites on here have another building he could lock?"

Ronin thought a minute, mentally reviewing his visits to the various locations. He'd been looking for scenery to photograph, not necessarily buildings, but since ruins added interest to his landscapes, he did make note of any that existed. "The ski area has an old lift shack, and it's near the highway."

"I'm very familiar with that one." Gage looked grim. "We had a serial killer take a hostage there a couple of years ago. It will be easy enough to check."

"There's a cabin here that is in pretty good shape." Ronin indicated another mine symbol. "But again, it's a long, grueling hike. A long way to go with a small child."

"We'll add it to the list," Gage said.

Ronin scanned the map again. Most of the other locations attracted visitors to collections of old scenery, the remains of tram towers, or particularly spectacular features. One had the remains of an old water-driven mill on the banks of a creek. He paused when he came to the name Grizzly Creek, and the familiar crossed pick and shovel emblem. "The Grizzly Creek mine is a possibility." Even as he said the words, a shiver raced up his spine. He had a clear picture in his head of the trio of carefully restored buildings that made up the site. "The Eagle Mountain Historical Society takes care of the site and they've restored several buildings. They're kept locked except for when the society holds tours, but it wouldn't be hard for someone to break the locks. And there's a good gravel road right up to the site." He met Gage's eyes across the table. "I think we should start there."

"I want to come with you," Courtney said.

"No." Gage shook his head. "No civilians. It's too dangerous."

"If Ashlyn is there, she'll be terrified," Courtney said. "She'll need me."

"We'll bring her to you as soon as possible," Gage said. "But we can't have you on-site."

"You can wait with Lauren," Ronin said. He glanced at the map again. "There's a café right here, where the road up to the site turns to gravel. If you and Lauren wait there you'll be close, but far enough away to be out of danger."

She opened her mouth to protest, but his hand on her arm silenced her. "It's the best you can do," he said. "We can't have a civilian near a potential hostage situation."

She pressed her lips together and nodded. "All right."

Gage began gathering up the maps. "I'm calling in the SWAT team from Montrose as backup," he said. "You've got ten minutes to change into tactical gear and meet back here."

Chapter Sixteen

Lauren and Courtney carried cups of coffee to a table by a side window, with a view of the road leading up the mountain, toward the old Grizzly Creek Mine. Every few minutes another law enforcement vehicle passed by, headed to the mine. "What if they're going to all this trouble for nothing?" Courtney asked. "Trey might not even be up there."

"Shane says the sheriff's department believes he hasn't left the county. Law enforcement across the state have been watching for him, plus most of his belongings were still at the trailer. They think he's hiding somewhere, waiting for an opportunity to slip away."

"Ronin said something similar," Courtney said. "But coming here is still just an educated guess. He could be anywhere."

"If he isn't here, they'll keep looking," Lauren said. "No one is going to give up."

Courtney nodded and sipped her coffee, her insides tied in knots. She hated being where she couldn't see what was going on.

"Have you ever eaten here?" Lauren asked, looking around them.

"No." The café advertised breakfast and lunch, and seemed to cater to backcountry hikers and skiers, and history buffs who came to tour the mine once a quarter during an open house hosted by the historical society. A small store adjacent to the dining room sold postcards, fishing lures, camping supplies and souvenirs. This morning the two women shared the space with a trio of men who talked fishing, a couple with soft Southern accents, and a single man who had a topo map spread on the table next to his BLT plate.

The door opened to admit a big man with thinning brown hair. His size—well over six feet and burly—attracted the attention of everyone in the restaurant, but the gun in a holster on his hip held that attention. He scanned the small dining room, then headed for Courtney and Lauren's table. "Hello," he said, stopping beside them. He held out a law enforcement ID. "Hello again, Ms. Baker. Do you remember me? Detective Fletcher. I'm working with Ronin Doyle on a case. He said you wouldn't mind answering a few questions for me."

Courtney had to crane her head to look up at him. She remembered the detective coming to the trailer with Ronin. "What kind of questions?" she asked.

"Just a few more things about Trey Allerton. As I mentioned before, we think he might be involved in a drug case Ronin and I are working on, in addition to everything else he's done."

Lauren moved over. "Sit down, Detective," she said. Fletcher sat, making the small table feel crowded.

Courtney wrapped her hands tightly around her coffee cup and told herself she had nothing to be nervous about. "I don't think I can help you, Detective," she said. "Trey was very secretive about all his activities."

"I saw all the sheriff's department vehicles headed up this way," he said. "Ronin said they were involved in an operation, but he didn't have time to give me much detail. Have they located Trey?"

"They're not sure," Courtney said. "They're looking at a number of locations where he might be hiding."

"What's up there?" Fletcher asked, nodding up the road.

"There's an old mine," Courtney said. "Some of the buildings have been restored. They think Trey might be hiding in one of them."

"He's been very good at hiding, hasn't he?" Detective Fletcher said. "Disguising himself, going under the name of Bart Smith. Did you know about all of that?"

"No. I didn't."

"Detective, I don't think you should be questioning Ms. Baker without her lawyer present," Lauren said.

"This is nothing formal," Fletcher said. "I'm just trying to get an idea of what Trey has been up to since he came here from Colorado Springs."

"The only thing I know is that he's been supervising the construction of buildings for a youth camp we planned to open." Courtney looked down into her coffee cup. "The camp was supposed to be to honor my husband. Trey raised a lot of money for it from local businesses and private donors. Though now I wonder how much of that money he kept for himself."

"Probably a lot of it," Fletcher said. "Your boyfriend was not an honest man, I know that."

"How do you know that?" Lauren asked.

"I used to be on the force in Colorado Springs. I know Allerton's history—though when I knew him, he went by the name Troy Allen."

Was he telling her Trey Allerton wasn't even the man's real name? Courtney closed her eyes. How had she been so naive?

"What do you think he's doing up there?" Fletcher asked.

She opened her eyes again, to find his fixed on her. The coldness of that stare frightened her. "I have no idea," she said. "And I don't really care. All I care about is getting my daughter back safely."

Fletcher scraped his chair back and rose. "I think I'll drive up there and see if I can help you do just that."

He left, and Lauren turned to stare after him. "He was at Ronin's gallery opening," she said. "He didn't stay long, but he and Ronin seemed friendly."

Courtney hadn't liked the detective, but maybe that was because his questions had reminded her yet again what a fool Trey Allerton had made of her. She watched Fletcher's car pull out of the parking lot and head up the road toward the mine. The place must be swarming with law enforcement by now. Surely if Trey was up there, he wouldn't slip past them this time.

By 11 A.M. Rayford County deputies had been at the mine for over an hour and the sheriff had assembled a team to assess the situation at the restored mine buildings. A SWAT team from Montrose and several officers from state patrol were on call to assist if it was determined Trey Allerton was hiding out in the buildings. "We're treating this as a potential hostage situation," Travis said to the group gathered around him at the far edge of the parking lot. "We're going to try to determine if any of the buildings are occupied, without alerting Allerton to our presence if possible." He glanced up toward the mine site, which wasn't visible from the parking area. "If we spot him, don't engage. We'll keep him surrounded and call for backup and a hostage negotiator."

"If he's in one of the buildings, he's going to be watching for anyone who might approach," Ronin said. "This is a popular area with tourists."

"We've sent up a drone to check out the area," Travis said. "Gage is operating it and he knows to stay up high, out of sight from the windows of the buildings." He looked to Ronin. "You say you're familiar with the area?"

"Yes, sir. I've taken photographs here several times."

"Give us an idea of what the layout is up there."

Ronin switched on his tablet and turned it toward the others. He'd assembled a slideshow of photos of the buildings. "There are three buildings," he said. "All situated on a bench of fairly level ground below the main shaft of the mine. The boardinghouse is the largest, on the east side." A picture of the boardinghouse, wood weathered dark brown from over a hundred years in the dry climate of the mountains, windows devoid of glass filling the front. "It's the least restored. Part of the floor is missing upstairs and all the windows. The structure has been stabilized and the roof and walls are solid, but it wouldn't be the most comfortable location to hide out."

He advanced to the next slide. "This is the assayer's office, roughly in the center of the complex. The front room has a museum display about the mine, with glass cases of artifacts and some antique furniture. The back room is empty."

The next slide showed a smaller building. "This was one of the homes for a mining supervisor. It's also two rooms, with a few pieces of furniture and some more informational displays. It's the only building with two doors—one in the front but another on the side near the back, with a shed roof built over it."

"Allerton would like the option of an escape hatch," Shane said.

"A wall of rock rises up very close behind this house," Ronin said. He advanced to a photo that showed more of the rock wall. "There's only about three feet between the back wall and the rock."

"How tall is that rock?" Dwight asked.

"Maybe three stories?" Ronin guessed. "There's a narrow ledge, then another rocky incline. I climbed up there once before and there was a lot of loose rock. It didn't feel very stable."

"What's the roof like?" Travis asked. "Any chance of getting in that way?"

"The historical society replaced all the roofs a couple of years ago," Ronin said. "They're metal and in good shape."

"Are there any windows on that back side?" Deputy Jamie Douglas asked.

Ronin thought a moment. "I can't remember," he said.

"I bet there isn't," Jamie said. "Why go to the trouble and expense if the only view was of a rock wall? Windows had to be hauled up here by burro, and they were expensive."

"Good to know," Travis said.

He looked up as Gage hurried toward them, carrying the drone. "I spotted what I think is Trey's truck," he said as soon as he was near enough to be heard without shouting. "It's tucked way back in the woods on the north side of the road about a mile from here." He set the drone on the ground beside him and switched on the controller, then angled the screen toward them.

Ronin studied the image on the screen, a dark bulk of what could have been a vehicle, mostly hidden by the feathery branches of evergreens. "I couldn't photograph the license plate, but it's definitely a black Ford truck," Gage said. "And whoever parked it there wanted to make sure it wasn't seen."

"Did you see any movement around any of the buildings?" Travis asked.

"No," Gage said. "I didn't see anyone. But if he's lying low in one of the buildings, I wouldn't expect to. There's a ridge up behind the buildings. If we can get someone up there, they'd have a good view of the whole place and they'd be out of sight of anyone in the buildings."

"Is there a trail up there?" Travis asked.

"There is," Ronin said. "Like I said, it's a lot of loose rock, but it's possible to hike up there."

"Anything else we should know about?" Travis asked.

"There's another vehicle parked down the road," Gage said. "Not far from the truck, but this one isn't hidden, just parked on the side. It wasn't there when I drove past when we first arrived. I couldn't get a good shot of the tag, though." He turned the screen on the controls toward them again.

Ronin felt a jolt as he studied the black sedan parked on the shoulder of the dirt road. "That looks like Jim Fletcher's car," he said.

"What's Jim Fletcher doing here?" Travis asked. "Did you tell him we were coming here?"

"No, sir," Ronin said. "I haven't talked to him."

"If he is here, why isn't he with us?" Gage asked. "Why is he parked a mile down the road? I didn't see anyone in the car."

"We'll deal with Fletcher if he shows up," Travis said. "Right now I want Ronin and Gage up on that ridge."

THE TRAIL TO the top of the ridge was rougher than Ronin remembered. In places the soil had collapsed, taking the trail with it. In other places, loose rock slid beneath their feet, so that he and Gage had to pick their way carefully. They moved as silently as possible, not wanting to raise any suspicions in Trey Allerton. Though they had still seen no sign of him, Ronin was more sure than ever that he was here.

It took them half an hour to reach the ridgetop. From there they could see the roofs of the three buildings below, as well as glimpse the part of the parking area below that and the law enforcement officers gathered there. Under other circumstances, it would have been a beautiful perspective of weathered buildings against a backdrop of red rock formations, dark green trees and robin's-egg blue sky. But the knowledge of the danger that might lay ahead tinted everything with foreboding.

Ronin pulled out a pair of binoculars and scanned the area below. Everything was still and eerily silent. "Travis is going to move men into the trees at the perimeter of the area," Gage said, speaking low, close to Ronin's ear. "We'll surround the place. He's also going to position a sharpshooter in the boardinghouse. Those upper windows ought to give a good view of the back door of the miner's house where we think Allerton is most likely to be."

Ronin turned his attention to the boardinghouse. The mining company had spared no expense building this lodging for its workers, importing enough windows that every room must have offered a view. Once the sharpshooter made his way up the decidedly unsafe stairway, he'd have his pick of vantage points from which to watch Allerton's supposed hideout.

Movement caught his eye—a man was making his way toward him, a tall man with broad shoulders. "Who is that?" Gage asked. "It's not Allerton."

"It's Jim Fletcher," Ronin said.

"What's he doing here?" Gage asked. "And why is he carrying that rifle?"

Fletcher had a rifle cradled in his arms. He moved swiftly toward them, more agile than Ronin would have guessed a man of his size could be.

"What are you doing here, Detective?" Gage asked, when Fletcher was close enough to hear the words, spoken just above a whisper.

"The same thing you are," Fletcher said. "I came for Trey Allerton." He glanced below. "Or as I knew him, Troy Allen."

"You told me you didn't know him," Ronin said.

"I didn't know Trey Allerton, but I knew Troy Allen very well." He lowered himself into a sitting position six feet from them, his back against the trunk of a twisted juniper. "Troy and I had dealings in Colorado Springs."

"Where you worked before," Ronin said.

Fletcher nodded. "That's right."

"We don't know for sure Allerton is here," Gage said.

"Oh, he's here," Fletcher said. "I saw him come out of the little house not ten minutes before you two climbed up here. He visited the outhouse. I would have taken him out then, but I couldn't get a good shot from where I was standing." He shifted the rifle in his arms. "He's back inside now."

"Did you see a little girl with him?" Ronin asked.

"If she's here, he left her in the house. Maybe she's tied up." He shrugged. "Maybe he already got rid of her."

His indifference sent a chill through Ronin.

"Rayford County Sheriff's Department is in charge

of this operation," Gage said. "If you want to be a part of it, you'll put that rifle away. You'll have your chance to question Allerton after we arrest him."

Fletcher said nothing, but remained focused on the scene below.

"How did you know we were here?" Ronin asked.

"I saw the sheriff's department vehicles headed this way. Then I stopped in at the little café at the bottom of the hill and Trey's girlfriend told me what you were up to." A smile played about the corner of his mouth. "I told her you said it was okay for her to talk to me."

Ronin glared at him, but now wasn't the time to get into it with the detective.

"Why did you park down the road?" Gage asked.

"I knew if I just showed up, you'd probably ask me to leave, or at least wait out of the way." He shifted the rifle again.

Ronin tensed. Something was very wrong with this situation. Should he mention he knew Fletcher had been suspended, or keep pretending he didn't know?

"There he is!" Fletcher leaned forward.

The front door of the cabin had opened and the top of Trey Allerton's head came into view. Fletcher raised the rifle to his shoulder.

"What are you doing?" Ronin hissed. "Put that down."

"I know you're out there!" Allerton shouted. "Don't try anything or I'll kill this little girl, I swear!"

Ashlyn's anguished cry stopped Ronin's heart for a beat, and then it began to race.

"Don't do anything stupid, Allerton!" Travis's voice, amplified by a bullhorn, came from the screen of trees.

"You're the one who shouldn't be stupid," Allerton said. "I want a free pass out of here. Call off the cops, let me go and you'll never hear from me again."

"Step out just a little bit more," Fletcher muttered. "Then we'll for sure never hear from you again."

"Put the gun down, Fletcher," Gage ordered.

Fletcher swiveled the gun to point at Gage. "Don't try to stop me," he said. "I'll kill you first, then I'll take care of Troy." He shifted his gaze to Ronin. "Don't you try anything, either."

"If you shoot at Trey, you could hit Ashlyn," Ronin said. "Or he could kill her before he dies."

"Maybe. It's a gamble I'm willing to take."

Fletcher still had his rifle trained on Gage. "Promise you won't interfere and I won't bother to shoot you later," he said. "I don't have a beef with you—this is between me and Troy."

"What's between you and Troy?" Ronin asked.

"You haven't figured that out?"

"Not all of it," Ronin hedged. "I know you've been suspended from the Delta Police Department. And I know you used to be with the Colorado Springs police."

"Then you don't know anything."

"Why were you suspended?" Gage asked.

"There were some…discrepancies in my account of my interactions with Dallas Keen. It will be cleared up soon enough."

"Did you kill Keen?" Ronin asked.

"No. Troy did that, I'm sure."

"Why would Troy kill him?" Ronin asked.

"I'm just guessing, but I think he was worried Keen knew too much about Bart Smith," Fletcher said. "And that he might tell me. Troy definitely didn't want me to know where he was or what he was doing these days."

"Troy was working for you in Colorado Springs," Ronin guessed. "Then he moved here and decided to strike out on his own." It explained Fletcher's interest in finding Trey, while pretending to focus on a broader case. It explained his suspension, too.

"I'm not going to say anything else," Fletcher said. He returned his attention to the scene below, though the rifle was still pointed toward them.

"He'll never move far enough away from the house for you to get a shot at him," Gage said, his tone conversational.

"He will if one of you goes down after him."

"That's a sheer wall," Ronin said.

"Not so steep if you go that way." Fletcher pointed farther down the trail. "It slopes almost down to the level of the boardinghouse over there," he said. "From there you can move along keeping close to the wall."

"Trey could see us," Ronin said.

"Only if you're careless. But if he does, it will draw him out so I can kill him."

"You're not the one in charge here, Fletcher," Gage said. "We're not going down there, to draw Trey out or for anything else."

"I'm not going to give you any choice," Fletcher said.

Gage didn't flinch. "You fire that rifle and you'll

have every cop within a quarter mile swarming up here. And you'll miss any chance of getting to Allerton."

Fletcher's finger hovered near the trigger of the rifle. "I told you—I'm a man who's willing to take chances," he said. "Are you? At this distance, a rifle bullet will blow right through any ballistics vest you're wearing."

Chapter Seventeen

Courtney pushed aside her now-cold coffee. It seemed as if she and Lauren had been waiting at this café for hours. The fishermen and the older couple had finished their meals, their places taken by a trio of young people in hiking gear and two more anglers. "I hate not knowing what's going on up there."

"It's hard, but we need to let the sheriff and his team handle this," Lauren said.

"If Trey is there with Ashlyn, I could talk to him," Courtney said. "He might let Ashlyn go if I promised him money, or if I said I'd go with him wherever he wanted."

Lauren clutched Courtney's wrist. "No! You don't mean that."

"I'd do it if it meant Ashlyn would be safe. You'd look after her, wouldn't you?"

Lauren withdrew her hand. "Of course I'd take care of Ashlyn, but you're not going to go back to Trey. Not after all the ways he's hurt you."

"I would do it to save Ashlyn," Courtney said. "It's my fault she's in danger now."

"It is not." Lauren deliberately softened her tone. "Give the sheriff and the deputies a chance to do the job they're trained and equipped for."

Courtney stared at the tabletop. Yes, the sheriff and his deputies had weapons and special training, but Trey hated cops. He was going to be hostile to them, no matter what. But Trey didn't hate her. He didn't respect her and he wanted to control her, but that wasn't the same as hate. She thought he'd probably taken Ashlyn because he wanted to get back at Courtney for leaving him.

If she could make him believe she would come back to him, he might let Ashlyn go free.

The waitress stopped by their table. "More coffee?" she asked.

"Yes, thanks." Lauren held out her cup, but Courtney shook her head.

When they were alone again, Courtney stood. "I have to go to the ladies' room," she said.

She could feel Lauren's eyes on her as she made her way down the short hallway to the women's restroom. At the end of the hall, the door was propped open to the kitchen, steam from the grill drifting out in a fragrant cloud. Beyond that, a second door led outside.

Lauren would say Courtney was being reckless. Foolish. Maybe she was both those things, but if anyone was going to reason with Trey, it had to be her.

Right now, she was Ashlyn's best chance, and she wasn't going to throw that away.

GAGE DIDN'T ANSWER Fletcher right away, but fixed him with a hard stare. Ronin's heart hammered, and he tried to focus on taking deep, slow breaths, fighting to remain focused and calm. Fletcher's face was flushed, his eyes bright. He looked excited. Aroused even—by the idea of killing a fellow officer? Ronin fought a sudden wave of nausea.

"I'll go down and try to draw out Allerton," Ronin said. At ground level, he could alert the others to Fletcher's presence, and get a better idea of what was going on with Ashlyn.

"Good idea," Gage said. He looked away from Fletcher, down toward the roof of the house where Trey waited. "We're not going to be able to do much from here."

"We can both go," Ronin said. Fletcher had suggested just that, before.

"The sergeant stays with me," Fletcher said. "A little insurance policy."

Ronin started to protest, but Gage shook his head. "Go on," he said.

Fletcher shoved himself to his feet to allow Ronin to pass. "Don't try anything clever or the sergeant is a dead man," he said.

"Allerton isn't going to come out just because I ask him to," Ronin said.

"Here." Fletcher reached into his pocket. "Take this." He tossed something to Ronin and Ronin caught what turned out to be a lighter. "Burn him out," Fletcher said. "That old cabin ought to catch fire like a pile of wooden matches."

"There's a child in there," Ronin said.

"I imagine Troy won't want to leave his hostage

behind," Fletcher said. "He'll bring her out believing she'll protect him from a frontal assault but he won't be expecting a shot from above."

Ronin said nothing. Fletcher wasn't behaving like any law enforcement officer he'd known.

"Get down there," Fletcher barked.

Ronin eased past Fletcher's bulk. He thought of trying to pull the bigger man off-balance, but the risk of the rifle firing or both of them falling to their deaths was too great.

He moved along the narrow trail, keeping away from the crumbling edge. He was sure Fletcher and Gage were watching him, but who else? Did any of the officers stationed below, their attention fixed on Trey Allerton's hideout, notice his movements above them? Could the officer in the boardinghouse see him? Or would they assume he was moving under orders from the sheriff or Gage?

The trail started to descend, and plunged into the cover of trees. Ronin looked back, unable to see Fletcher or Gage anymore. That should mean they couldn't see him. He stopped, back against a tree, and took stock of the situation.

Fletcher wanted him to set fire to the old cabin—a 140-year-old building that had been carefully restored by the local historical society. A building that contained a three-year-old who might be injured and even killed by a blaze. There had to be another way to get Trey Allerton away from Ashlyn. But once Allerton stepped away from that cabin, Fletcher intended to kill him—and maybe any officer who tried to interfere.

He moved closer to the cabin. If he could get into it through that side door, he might be able to surprise Allerton and overpower him.

The trail ended behind the boardinghouse. From there, Ronin kept to the cover of rock and trees, slowly making his way toward the cabin. How much time had passed since Trey had emerged to make his demands? Was he growing restless? Would he try to make a break for it, or try to put more pressure on law enforcement by hurting Ashlyn?

Ronin had just reached the assayer's office when movement in the woods to his left made him freeze. Twenty yards ahead of him a shadowy figure was also moving toward the cabin.

Ronin caught up with the sheriff approximately fifty feet from the cabin's side door, in the shelter of a pile of rocks that had fallen from the cliff above at some point in the past. Travis didn't seem surprised to see him.

"I thought that was you," Travis said. He focused binoculars on the cabin. "What's up?"

"Jim Fletcher is above us with a rifle," Ronin said. "He's holding it on Gage and he sent me down to set fire to the cabin. He plans to shoot Allerton when he runs out to escape the flames."

Travis's mouth tightened, though he remained focused on the cabin. "What's Fletcher's angle?"

"He says he knew Trey Allerton as Troy Allen in Colorado Springs. Apparently, he has a score to settle with him."

"He'll have to settle it later." Travis lowered the binoculars and stowed them in a pocket. "And no one's setting anything on fire."

"No, sir. I wasn't planning on it."

"Have you been inside this cabin?" Travis asked. "What's the layout?"

"I went on one of the tours once. This door opens in a lean-to that was added after the original construction. It's maybe six feet long and five feet wide, with hooks on the wall for coats. A second door from there opens into a kitchen."

"The door's probably locked," Travis said.

"It is when they're not running tours," Ronin said. "But Trey must have unlocked it. Fletcher said he went out that way to use the outhouse less than an hour ago."

Travis glanced at the outhouse that stood between the cabin and the assayer's office, behind a section of wooden fencing, then returned his attention to the cabin. "So there's a chance he didn't lock it again."

"He'd want that way open in case he had to duck out quickly," Ronin said.

Travis nodded. "You can cover me while I go in," he said.

"Or you could cover me while I go in. Ashlyn knows me," he added at Travis's dark look.

The sheriff glanced overhead. "I haven't heard anything from up there."

"Fletcher is probably waiting for smoke and flames."

Travis drew his Glock. "You wait here," he said. "I may send Ashlyn out to you."

"Yes, sir."

Travis started toward the cabin, but before he had taken five steps, a woman's voice froze him in place.

"Trey! Trey, it's me, Courtney. I'm sorry I left you. Please come out and talk to me."

COURTNEY HAD PLENTY of time to think about what she was doing on the long walk up to the old mine site. At first, she'd been afraid someone would see her and force her to turn back. Then she had realized that if that was the worst anyone could do, she really had nothing to be afraid of. She would either realize her goal of talking to Trey or she wouldn't, but at least she would have tried to save her daughter. If she sat at that café and waited for other people to act she didn't think she would be able to live with herself if Ashlyn ended up hurt.

No one stopped her on the road, or when she reached the parking area. She spotted a few officers waiting near their vehicles, but none of them noticed her. Everyone was focused on a cabin at the end of the row of buildings, so she was able to slip past them. No one knew she was there until she walked out into the clearing and shouted for Trey to come out.

"Trey! Trey, it's me, Courtney. I'm sorry I left you. Please come out and talk to me."

She waited, silence pressing in around her, as if everyone was holding their breath. Was Trey ignoring her? Was he not there?

The door of the cabin creaked as it opened, not enough for her to see inside, only an inch or so. "What are you doing, Courtney?" Trey asked, his voice eerily calm, as if he was sitting at the kitchen table while she prepared dinner.

"I...I wanted to see you again," she said. "I was wrong to leave you. Can you forgive me?"

"Why should I forgive you? It's your fault I'm in this mess."

"I know, Trey. I'm sorry." She had said the same words so many times before. Now that she didn't mean them, they were harder to force out. She smiled, trying to make the expression as warm and genuine as possible. Forget photography classes—she should take up acting. "Between the two of us, we can figure this out," she said. "You always said we make a great team."

"I don't need you now," Trey said. "I've got Ashlyn."

"How is Ashlyn?" She hoped he wouldn't notice the way her voice broke on the name. She raised her voice. "Ashlyn, honey, Mommy's here!"

She heard a noise in the cabin—was that Ashlyn? "Let me see her, Trey," she said. "Please." She would beg him on her knees, if that's what he wanted. She had no pride when it came to her child.

No answer came for a long, agonizing moment. She took a few steps closer to the cabin, and was about to call out again when the door eased open a few more inches and Ashlyn was there. Trey was holding her in front of him, so that she almost completely blocked the lower half of his body. But her little girl was there!

"Mama!" Ashlyn called, and held out her arms.

"Oh, sweetie, Mommy's here." She took a few steps closer, and Ashlyn began to cry. Before Courtney could reach her, the door shut again.

"Trey!" Courtney pounded on the door. "Let me in, please."

"Go away," he called.

"No! I want to be with my baby."

"You don't deserve her," Trey said. "You don't deserve either of us."

There had been a time when his words would have hurt her deeply, but she scarcely registered them now. This wasn't about her. It was about getting Ashlyn away from him.

She looked around, taking stock of the situation. A couple of uniformed deputies had moved out of the cover of the trees to stand at the edge of the clearing. One of them motioned for her to join them, but she shook her head and turned back to face the cabin.

"Trey, what are you going to do?" she asked. "You're trapped in there. I can help you."

"I'm not stupid," he said, and for the first time she heard frustration in his voice. "I know they sent you to trick me. I don't need your help. I've got Ashlyn. As long as I have her, they have to let me walk out of here."

"Please open the door so we can talk," she said.

"And give one of their snipers a shot at me? I won't do it."

"You don't have to show yourself," she said. "Just open it a little, like before. So we can have a conversation. We'll figure this out. We always have before."

She waited another long beat, and then the door eased open. She couldn't see Trey—only the gap between the door and the frame. But when he spoke, his voice was clearer. "Tell the cops to back off," he said.

She turned toward the officers behind her. "Please back off," she said.

They stared at her a long moment, then melted back into the woods. She faced the cabin once more.

"They moved back," she said. "Will you let me come in with you?" She had to get to Ashlyn. She had to make sure her baby was all right.

"If I let you in here, you won't leave again," Trey said. "I'll make sure of it."

The words sent a chill through her. She knew what he meant. This time, Trey would kill her before he let her leave. But she couldn't walk away now. She couldn't abandon her daughter again. What choice did she have?

RONIN'S STOMACH TWISTED when Courtney asked Trey to forgive her. She didn't really want to go back to him, did she? He couldn't decide if her being here was incredibly foolish—or incredibly brave. It didn't matter, because now they had two people to protect—her and Ashlyn.

"We've got to make our move before she goes in there with him," Travis said, his voice barely audible.

Ronin nodded.

"If she'll keep him talking, we can rush the cabin from this side," Travis said. "You grab the girl and I'll take care of Trey."

"Yes, sir." Ronin focused on the door, trying to remember what the interior of the cabin looked like. There wasn't a lot of furniture, or many places for a child to hide. But they wouldn't have much time. They needed to hit hard and fast, and be in and out before bullets started flying.

"He's got the kid now," Travis said, and Ronin's heart sank. Their plan of attack wasn't going to work if Trey was holding Ashlyn, using her as a shield.

They listened to the conversation between Trey and Courtney. There was no mistaking the desperation in her voice after Trey shut the door in her face.

"We should go now," Ronin said.

Travis put a hand on his chest, stopping him. "Wait."

They waited. And then Trey was talking again, agreeing to open the door a little.

"Now," Travis said, and sprinted toward the cabin.

Ronin ran after him. Travis reached the door, pulled it open, and then they were in, the dark of the windowless lean-to disorienting after the bright sunlight. But they kept pushing forward, through the second door and inside.

Trey turned toward them, and fumbled for the gun at his side, but Travis had already tackled him, bringing him to his knees, then facedown onto the floor.

"Ashlyn!" Ronin called for the girl, and when she cried out in response he whirled to find her cowering on the bunk in the corner, a blanket clutched to her chest.

He forced himself to approach slowly, dimly aware of Travis handcuffing Trey and talking to him. Ronin crouched in front of the bunk. "Hello, Ashlyn," he said. "Do you remember me? It's your mom's friend, Ronin."

Ashlyn, eyes so big in her pale little face, nodded.

"Would you like to go see your mother?" He extended one hand. "Come here and I'll take you to her."

Ashlyn came to him, still clutching the blanket. He pulled her into his arms and stood.

The front door to the cabin burst open and a trio of officers entered. "Take him," Travis said, and they hustled Trey toward the door.

Ronin started to follow, but just then a single rifle shot echoed over the clearing, and all the color drained from the sheriff's face. "Gage," he said.

"Fletcher," Ronin said. In the chaos he had forgotten all about the detective and the sergeant. Had Fletcher shot Gage Walker after all?

"Keep Trey and Ashlyn in the cabin," Travis said, then headed out the door, running toward the trail that led to the top of the rock wall. Ronin handed Ashlyn to one of the other officers, then took off after Travis, praying they weren't too late.

Chapter Eighteen

Ronin and Travis were halfway up the trail when Fletcher's bellow rang over the area, a string of profanity and protest. The two men ran faster, then slowed at the top, where Fletcher lay prone on the ground, hands cuffed behind his back, Gage standing over him with the rifle, blood pouring from a cut on one side of his face. Gage looked up at their approach. "As soon as you hauled Allerton into view, Fletcher tried to get off a shot. I managed to knock the rifle away and the shot went wild."

"You're bleeding." Travis touched his own temple.

Gage wiped at the blood. "He picked up a rock and clocked me, but I got off a good punch. I think I broke his nose."

The three of them turned to Fletcher, who glared up at them. His face was bloody, too. "Why did you want to shoot Allerton?" Travis asked.

Fletcher looked away and said nothing.

"Let's get him up and out of here," Travis said. He and Ronin hauled Fletcher to his feet and walked him down the trail, Gage following. When they reached ground level, they turned Fletcher over to two other deputies and returned to the cabin. "Put Allerton in a vehicle and take the little girl to her mother," Travis said.

Back outside, they found two more deputies restraining a struggling Courtney. "I have to get to my daughter!" she protested.

"It's okay," Ronin said. "Ashlyn is right here. It's okay, guys," he added.

Deputies Dwight Prentice and Jamie Douglas stopped struggling with Courtney, then released their hold on her and stepped back. She ran to him, and took Ashlyn from him. Both mother and child were sobbing now. Ashlyn put her arms around her mother's neck and buried her face against Courtney's shoulder. Courtney rocked the little girl back and forth and kissed her over and over. She never even looked at Ronin. He could have been a thousand miles away.

Ronin followed Travis and Gage away from the cabin. They were halfway across the compound when Courtney approached, Ashlyn in her arms. "Thank you," she said. Though she spoke to all of them, her gaze was on Ronin. "Thank you for saving my little girl."

"I could charge you with interfering with a law enforcement operation," Travis said.

"I knew Trey wouldn't be able to resist talking to me," she said. "Especially if I could make him believe I wanted to come back to him."

"Did you want that?" Ronin asked.

Her eyes widened. "No! Never! I only said that so he'd listen to me, and keep talking."

"You distracted him so we could get to him, so we won't be charging you," Travis said. "But you took a dangerous risk."

"What will happen to Trey now?" she asked.

"He'll be charged with kidnapping Ashlyn, and probably a number of other crimes."

"Will he be released on bail?" She bit her lip.

"I think that's very unlikely," Travis said.

Her shoulders sagged. "That's good."

"What will you do now?" Ronin asked.

"Ashlyn and I will stay with Lauren until we figure that out," Courtney said.

"Ronin, give Ms. Baker a ride back to the café," Travis said.

"Yes, sir."

Neither he nor Courtney spoke on the way back to the parking lot. Once there, she stared across to where Trey was just visible in the back seat of a sheriff's department SUV. "I was terrified while I was standing there talking to him," she said. "I was so afraid he'd hurt Ashlyn."

"You weren't afraid he'd hurt you?" Ronin asked.

She gathered Ashlyn closer. "He's hurt me before and I survived."

The bleakness of that statement—as if she deserved, or at least expected, to be hurt—made him ache for her. "Come on," he said. "You must be exhausted."

He helped her settle Ashlyn in the back seat. At the last minute, he remembered the stuffed bears they carried to hand out to traumatized children and took one out. "I have a new friend for you, Ashlyn," he said, and offered the bear.

She beamed and reached for the bear. "What do you say?" Courtney asked.

"Thank you." Ashlyn hugged the bear. "I'm going to call him Paul."

"Why Paul?" Courtney asked.

Ashlyn looked stern. "Because that's his name."

Courtney slid into the front passenger seat and fastened her seat belt and they set out, but they hadn't gone far when Courtney asked him to pull over. "I need a minute," she said. "Before I face Lauren. She's going to be furious with me, I know."

He pulled over onto the side of the road, but left the engine running. When he looked over, she had her head back, her eyes closed. She opened them and met his gaze full on. "You're dying to say something," she said. "So say it."

"You weren't the only one who was terrified while you were talking to Trey," he said. "I couldn't believe it when I saw you."

"I'm not going to apologize for trying to save my daughter." She clenched her hands in her lap. "I've spent most of my life letting other people—my parents, then my husband, then Trey—do everything for me. I'm trying very hard to learn to make my own decisions." She gave a shaky laugh. "It's not as easy as you might think."

"I'm not criticizing you," he said. He put his arm along the seat, his fingers near, but not touching her.

He didn't dare. He didn't want to deal with the hurt if she rebuffed him.

She looked at him finally, a pleading look. "I need time to process all this," she said.

He nodded and withdrew his hand. "Of course." Maybe he needed time, too, to figure out what his feelings were for this complicated woman.

Lauren greeted them in the parking lot of the café. "I've been so worried. What happened?" Then she saw Ashlyn, and tears spilled down her face. "Ashlyn, honey, you're all right." The two women and the child embraced. Ronin started to turn away, but Lauren called after him. "Ronin, wait."

"Yes?"

Lauren left Courtney and Ashlyn and caught up with him. "What happened to Trey?" she asked.

"He's under arrest."

"Was anyone hurt?"

"No."

She closed her eyes. "Thank God."

"I have to get back." He glanced toward Courtney, who was focused on Ashlyn. "Don't give her too much grief about going after Trey," he said. "She's had a tough time of it."

"I know," Lauren said. "To tell the truth, I admire her determination. Though she took a terrible risk."

"It was a risk, but it worked out. She distracted Trey long enough that we could get to him and arrest him."

"I'm just glad this is all over." She turned back to Courtney and Ronin returned to his vehicle. The adrenaline of the moment had drained away, leaving him exhausted and deflated. He tried to focus on the work that lay ahead. He had a job to do, and nothing would come of fretting over tomorrow or next week when there was so much to deal with right now.

Back at the sheriff's department, Travis waylaid him. "I want to talk to Fletcher first," he said. "I'd like you to sit in, since you can fill in details the rest of us may not know."

Fletcher hunched over the table in the interview room, his nose taped, dark bruises under both eyes. He glared at them when they entered, but said nothing. Travis read off the information for the recording and repeated the Miranda warning. "Do you understand your rights?" he asked.

"I understand I don't have to talk to you," Fletcher said.

"No, you don't have to say anything to us," Travis said. "Have you contacted an attorney, or do you need us to provide one for you?"

Silence.

Travis sat across from Fletcher. "I've spoken with your supervisor at Delta PD and he tells me you're on administrative leave, pending an investigation into your possible connection with a drug ring operating in the area," Travis said. "A drug operation that may have originated in Colorado Springs, when you worked there. Is that how you came to know Trey Allerton, aka Troy Allen?"

Fletcher remained silent.

"We have reason to believe you and Allerton worked together on that Colorado Springs operation," Travis said. "We'll be contacting your former supervisors there to fill in the blanks about that. And we'll be talking to Allerton."

"If Allen says we worked together, he's lying," Fletcher said.

"Trey Allerton has indicated he's very eager to talk to us," Travis said. "He's especially eager to tell us everything he knows about you."

"He's a liar. You ought to know that by now."

"Is that why you were so eager to put a bullet in him?" Travis asked. "Because you didn't want him revealing what he knows about you?"

Fletcher's eyes burned with hatred, but he said nothing.

After several more questions, to which they received no reply, Travis stood. "You'll appear before the district judge tomorrow morning. You should arrange for representation before then."

A deputy arrived to transport Fletcher back to his cell. When they were alone and the recording was off, Travis asked, "What do you think?"

"I don't know what to think," Ronin said. "He definitely hates Trey, but no cop with any experience would say a word without his lawyer present, whether he's guilty or innocent."

"Let's see what Allerton has to say," Travis said. "I've asked for him to be brought up."

"Did he really say he wanted to talk to us?" Ronin asked.

"He seems very eager."

Trey looked tired and disheveled, but he smiled at

them when he entered the interview room and sat up
straight in his chair, some of his old charm visible beneath the weariness. Travis went through the routine
for the recording. When Travis asked if Trey understood his rights, he said yes. "I'm happy to help you
any way I can," he added.

"Do you wish to have a lawyer present?" Travis
asked.

"I don't think that's necessary. I don't have anything to hide."

"Tell us how you know Jim Fletcher," Travis said.

"I met Detective Fletcher in Colorado Springs. He
asked me to help him with an investigation."

"What kind of investigation?"

"He was trying to infiltrate a drug ring. He asked
me to pretend to be interested in working with the ring
and to report back to him, so I did."

"You went undercover at Fletcher's direction?"
Travis asked.

Trey smiled. "I did. My hobby was amateur theat-
rics, and I'm a pretty good actor, plus I already knew
some of the people involved."

"And how long were you involved in this investigation of Fletcher's?"

"Nine months? Until Detective Fletcher left the Colorado Springs Police Department. I had no idea he had
moved to Delta."

"The two of you didn't keep in touch?"

"We had no reason to."

"He says he knew you as Troy Allen."

"Yeah, that's the name I gave him in Colorado

Springs. I guess even then I didn't entirely trust him. I figured it was safer not to use my real name."

"What do you know about Dallas Keen?" Travis shifted the conversation.

Trey blinked. "Who?"

"He was a teenager Fletcher said was part of a drug operation in Delta. His body was found not far from here, in Rayford County."

"I don't know anything about him. I didn't even know there was a drug operation in Delta. I mean, why would I?"

"Supposedly, this group recruits teenagers to distribute drugs for them."

Trey nodded. "Fletcher did some of that in Colorado Springs. I guess the kids were easy to frighten into not saying anything, and if they were caught, they got light sentences because they were juveniles."

"Wait a minute," Travis said. "You said Detective Fletcher was investigating a drug ring in Colorado Springs."

Trey's expression grew more serious. "That's what he told me—and I presume his bosses. But when I got in deeper, I figured out he was really behind the whole thing. That's another reason I wanted to get away from having anything to do with him."

"So you were completely innocent," Travis said. "A dupe."

"I guess you could say that." He looked contrite. "One of my flaws is that I really do think the best of people. It's led to some poor choices in friends in the past."

"Tell us about Bart Smith," Travis said.

Trey's expression never faltered. "Who?"

"The name you used when you dressed up and harassed Cash Whitlow, for example," Travis said. "You tried to kill him."

"I never tried to kill anyone. I'm a nonviolent person."

"Jim Fletcher says Bart Smith was the one who recruited young people for the drug ring in Delta. According to witnesses, Dallas Keen was seen with Bart Smith only a few hours before he was murdered."

"I don't know anyone named Bart Smith. And Fletcher is lying. That shouldn't surprise you. He's trying to protect himself."

"We found the trunk in your shed with all the clothing Bart Smith was described as wearing, along with wigs and other disguises."

"I don't know anything about that."

"Then how did the items get in your shed?"

"They were on the property when we moved in. I don't know who they belonged to."

"We found the gold you took from Martin Kramer."

"I didn't take it. Mr. Kramer donated the gold to my youth camp."

"Why would he do that?"

"I think his conscience was bothering him after he killed that climber." Trey shrugged. "I was happy to get the donation, so I didn't question him."

"He says different. He says the gold was stolen."

"Well, he would say that, wouldn't he?"

Trey Allerton had an answer for everything, deliv-

ered with such confidence people who didn't know better might be inclined to believe him. Was this how he
had persuaded Courtney, who was smart but maybe a
little naive, to trust him?

"Why did you kidnap Ashlyn Baker?" Travis asked.

"I didn't kidnap her." Trey managed to look offended. "I love Ashlyn, and she adores me."

"You took her from her mother and said it was in
retaliation for Ms. Baker leaving you."

"That was a misunderstanding. I took Ashlyn because I found her wandering by herself in the middle
of nowhere. Clearly, she wasn't safe with her mother."

Ronin wanted to argue that that was not what had
happened, but he forced himself to keep quiet. Trey
leaned across the table toward the sheriff. "Courtney
is a very sweet woman, but she's mentally and emo-
tionally unstable. I did my best to look after her, but in
the end, I had to put the needs of Ashlyn ahead of my
feelings for Courtney. I was trying to protect the child."

"You held the child hostage in that cabin and tried
to use her as a shield when confronted with law enforcement."

"Another misunderstanding," Trey said. He sat up
straighter. "I've answered enough questions now. I see
how things are. You've already assumed I'm guilty. I'm
done talking to you."

"He's still trying to charm his way out of trouble,"
Ronin said when he and Travis were alone again.

"Yep," Travis said. "Even a crooked cop isn't going
to 'recruit' a civilian for undercover work. And no one

could believe Allerton is as naive about people as he likes to pretend."

"Courtney isn't unstable," Ronin said. "And Ashlyn was very happy to be reunited with her."

"We've got our work cut out for us, but we're going to prove Trey Allerton is guilty—of kidnapping and theft, and possibly even murder," Travis said. "We're going to look into his involvement with Jim Fletcher and with drug dealing. His charm isn't going to do him much good when we have all the facts."

"Yes, sir." Ronin wanted to be a part of making Trey pay for all the crimes he had committed. But what about all the harm he had done to Courtney and her child? Would they ever heal from the wounds he had inflicted?

And would Courtney ever look at Ronin and not see the lawman who had been a part of what must have been one of the worst ordeals of her life?

Chapter Nineteen

Courtney didn't see Ronin for the next two weeks. At first she was so absorbed in taking care of Ashlyn and trying to figure out the next steps for her own life that she didn't have too much time to brood over the handsome lawman.

Then she wondered if Ronin was avoiding her. She couldn't blame him if he didn't want anything to do with a woman who had voluntarily lived with a criminal. Maybe he didn't believe her when she told him she had been lying to Trey about wanting to be with him again.

One Saturday afternoon, approximately two weeks after the ordeal at the cabin, Courtney was folding clothes while Lauren read the newspaper. "Did you see this story about Trey?" Lauren asked.

The name startled Courtney so much she dropped the pair of socks she had been rolling into a ball. "What about him? He's not out on bail, is he?"

"Not hardly. Apparently, they've got two witnesses who have identified him as a key figure in a drug ring that operated in both Colorado Springs and Delta

County. And a Delta police detective was involved in the drug dealing, too. A Detective Jim Fletcher." Lauren frowned. "Was that the man who stopped and talked to us at the café?"

"Yes." Courtney came over to Lauren's chair and looked over her shoulder. "What else does the article say?"

"They've linked Trey to the death of a teenager he recruited to sell drugs for him, as well as stolen gold bars. The bars belonged to a local miner, Martin Kramer." She scanned down the page. "And they've linked a gun that belonged to Trey to the shooting of a climber who was found dead in his RV. It says here Trey's shot didn't kill the young man, but he could be charged with tampering with a deceased body." She looked up at Courtney. "Did you have any idea Trey was involved with all that?"

"No." She shook her head.

Lauren folded the paper and set it aside. "It sounds like he's going to be in prison for a long time, with all these charges. You could probably sue him for all the money he conned out of you."

"What would be the point?" Courtney asked. "It's not as if I could get any of the money back. I just want to put all of this behind me."

Lauren squeezed her hand. "And you're doing a great job of it. I'm really proud of you."

"I still have more to do," Courtney said.

"Are you talking about the youth camp?"

Courtney shook her head. "Now that I know that wasn't really Mike's dream, my heart isn't in the project. I have other things to do, more mistakes to make up for."

"Don't be so hard on yourself," Lauren said. "And you don't have to change everything overnight. Shane and I are happy to have you stay with us as long as you like."

"I'm meeting with a real estate agent next week to look at rental properties," Courtney said. "I'm nervous about being on my own, but I think it's time." She glanced at the paper. Later, she would read the article about Trey, but now she needed to take care of something else. Something she had been putting off too long. "Would you mind watching Ashlyn for a couple of hours?" she asked. "I need to run an errand."

"Sure. Take your time."

Courtney drove across town in the used Subaru she had purchased just last week. It felt good to have her own vehicle again—one more step in her independence.

But looking after herself didn't mean cutting ties with everyone who was important to her. She had been waiting for Ronin to contact her, but maybe he was waiting for her to make the first move. The only way she was ever going to find out what his feelings for her were was to ask. She might not like the answers he gave, but at least she would know, and she'd be able to move on.

She parked in front of his house, then hurried to the door before she lost courage. She waited on his front step after knocking, trying not to fidget. She told herself she had nothing to be nervous about. This was

Ronin. Her friend. Her lover. But it felt as if so much was riding on this moment.

The door opened and her heart jumped at the sight of him. He didn't seem as moved, his expression guarded. "Hello, Courtney. How are you doing?"

"I'm good," she said. "Can I come in?"

"Of course." He stood aside and as she moved past him she caught the scent of him—herbal shampoo and soap and soft cotton.

"You cut your hair," he said.

She put a hand to the new short style, which still felt so strange. "I wanted a change," she said.

He nodded. "It looks good. Lighter."

She felt lighter, but not just because of the hair.

"Come sit down." He led her to the sofa, and moved aside a stack of books to make room for her at one end. He sat beside her, but not too close. "I've been meaning to get in touch with you."

"Oh?" Again, that wild leap of her heart.

"We've learned some things in the course of our investigation that I wanted you to know. I know you blamed yourself for upsetting Trey, which led to him kidnapping Ashlyn. But I don't think that was the only reason he acted so rashly that day."

"Then what do you think was the reason?"

"Jim Fletcher had been hunting him. That day he and I came to your trailer to question Trey—I think Fletcher was beginning to suspect Trey was the Troy Allen who had double-crossed him. The next day I saw Fletcher talking to a man in an alleyway in Eagle Mountain. I couldn't see who it was, but after Fletcher left, I was sure I saw Ashlyn peeking out of the alley. I think Trey had sent her to check that the coast was clear. When she spotted me, the two of them slipped into the back door of one of the stores that opened onto the alley. I think Fletcher probably threatened Trey, so Trey was desperate to get away. He probably saw you and Ashlyn as his ticket to freedom."

She nodded. "Trey was definitely agitated when he came home that afternoon. I thought it was because he had found out I'd taken some of his stash of gold bars."

"Those bars were definitely stolen from Martin Kramer," Ronin said. "They'll be returned to his daughter."

"Trey had the gold, and all the money he had taken from me and gotten from donors, and he still wanted more."

"He probably realized we were getting suspicious of his plans for the camp. After he was arrested, we contacted some of the people he had listed as staff for the camp. None of them had ever heard of him. He was using that list of experts he had supposedly hired for the camp to entice donors."

"So the camp was just another scam?" she asked. "He never intended to open it at all?"

"It looks that way," Ronin said.

Then Trey had probably been lying about Mike wanting to build the youth camp. Lauren had said before that she didn't think Trey and Mike were friends. They had served together, and Trey had somehow gotten that picture of Courtney. He must have targeted her for a scam from the beginning. The idea made her feel sick. She was going to need time to come to terms with all the lies she had fallen for. "I had no idea of any of this."

"He purposely kept you in the dark." He shifted, and his expression softened. "Tell me what you've been up to."

"I've been busy," she said. "I have an appointment with a real estate agent next week to look at some rentals, and I'm enrolling Ashlyn in a local preschool. She needs to make friends with other children."

"So you're staying here, in Eagle Mountain?"

"Yes." It hurt that he would think otherwise, but she pushed past that. "Lauren has given me the name of a family therapist she says is good—I'm going to make an appointment for Ashlyn and me to see her. And I'm going to use some of the money from my trust to go back to school. To study graphic design and photography."

"I'm glad. You'll do great, but if you need any help with the photography…"

She took his hand in both of hers. "I'm counting on you to give me some pointers," she said.

He looked down at her hands wrapped around his, but didn't try to pull away. "I'll be happy to help any way I can."

She scooted closer to him. "I don't want your help," she said. "Or not only your help. I want…well, I hope we can continue to see each other."

His eyes met hers, still wary. "I wasn't sure how you'd feel about me, considering we met at such a difficult time in your life."

"You've been a true friend to me—one of the truly good things to come out of all of this. I'm not going to throw that away." She scooted closer still, their thighs touching. "I really like you, Ronin. A great deal. But I'm wary of rushing into anything. I need time to get my life together, to figure out who I am when I'm not defining myself as someone's daughter or wife or girl-friend. I want us to back up a little and take the time to get to know each other—to date and hang out and grow together. I need you to be patient with me."

"I can do that." He brought their clasped hands to his lips and kissed her knuckles. "One of the things a good photographer needs is patience. I spend a lot of time waiting for clouds to shift or the light to be just right. I'm good at waiting."

She tugged her hands out of his grasp, but only to reach up and pull his face down to hers. As soon as their lips touched she melted against him, the banked-up longing of the past few days finding its escape. He responded with the same ardor, his lips firm and sensu-ous, his tongue teasing and coaxing, leaving her giddy and breathless.

Reluctantly, she pulled away. "I have to go," she whispered. "Lauren is watching Ashlyn and I feel like I've imposed on her too much already. But I'll see you again soon. When I can stay longer."

His smile sent a fresh thrill through her—warm and a little wicked, promising good things to come. "I'll look forward to it," he said, then stood and pulled her up alongside him. "You've given me a lot to look for-ward to."

"Me, too." She kissed him again, a brief brush of her lips to his, then turned away. There would be more kisses, more conversation, more learning to know each other as the best of friends and the truest of lovers. Not that long ago she had thought she would never know this feeling again. Now it was a wonderful gift. One she intended to savor, and nurture, so that it lasted a lifetime.

* * * * *

Look for more books from Cindi Myers coming soon!

And if you missed the previous stories in the Eagle Mountain: Search for Suspects miniseries, look for:

Disappearance at Dakota Ridge
Conspiracy in the Rockies
Missing at Full Moon Mine

Available now wherever Harlequin Intrigue books are sold!

#2067 SNIFFING OUT DANGER
K-9s on Patrol • by Elizabeth Heiter

When former big-city cop Ava Callan stumbles upon a bomb, she seizes the chance to prove herself to the small-town police department where she's becoming a K-9 handler...but especially to charming lead investigator Eli Thorne. The only thing more explosive than her chemistry with the out-of-town captain? The danger menacing them at every turn...

#2068 UNDERCOVER COUPLE
A Ree and Quint Novel • by Barb Han

Legendary ATF agent Quint Casey isn't thrilled to pose as Ree Sheppard's husband for a covert investigation into a weapons ring that could be tied to his past. But when his impetuous "wife" proves her commitment to the job, Quint feels a spark just as alarming as the dangerous killers he's sworn to unmask.

#2069 DODGING BULLETS IN BLUE VALLEY
A North Star Novel Series • by Nicole Helm

When the attempted rescue of his infant twins goes horribly wrong, Blue Valley sheriff Garret Averly and North Star doctor Betty Wagner take the mission into their own hands. Deep in the Montana mountains and caught in a deadly storm, he's willing to sacrifice everything to bring Betty and his children home safely.

#2070 TO CATCH A KILLER
Heartland Heroes • by Julie Anne Lindsey

Apprehending a violent fugitive is US marshal Nash Winchester's top priority when Great Falls chef Lana Iona becomes the next target as the sole eyewitness to a murder. Forced to stay constantly on the move, can the Kentucky lawman stop a killer from permanently silencing the woman he's never forgotten?

#2071 ACCIDENTAL AMNESIA
The Saving Kelby Creek Series • by Tyler Anne Snell

Awakening in an ambulance headed to Kelby Creek, Melanie Blankenship can't remember why or how she got there. While she's back in the town that turned on her following her ex-husband's shocking scandal, evidence mounts against Mel in a deadly crime. Can her former love Deputy Sterling Costner uncover the criminal before she pays the ultimate price?

#2072 THE BODY IN THE WALL
A Badge of Courage Novel • by Rita Herron

The sooner Special Agent Macy Stark can sell her childhood home, the sooner she can escape her small town and shameful past—until she discovers a body in the wall and her childhood nightmares return. Handsome local sheriff Stone Lawson joins the cold case—but someone will stop at nothing to keep the past hidden.

"I wouldn't have bought the place if I'd known you would ever
come back here to live," she explained. "You always said you'd
get out and stay out, come hell or high water."

Yeah, he'd indeed said that all right. Now he was eating
those words. "Anything else going on with you that I should
know about?"

"I'm making Natalie's wedding dress," she readily admitted.

Maybe she thought she'd see some disapproval on his face
over that. She wouldn't. Matt didn't necessarily buy into the
bunk about Emory's dresses being *mostly lucky*, but he wanted
Natalie to be happy. Because that in turn would improve Jack's
chances of being happy. If Vince Parkman and Last Ride were
what Natalie needed for that happiness, then Matt was willing to
give the man, and the town, his blessing.

"Anything else?" he pressed. "I'd like not to get blindsided
by something else for at least the next twenty-four hours."

Emory cocked her head to the side, studying him again.

Then smiling. Not a big beaming smile but one with a sly edge to it. "You mean like nightly loud parties, nude gardening or weddings in the pasture?"

Of course, his brain, and another stupid part of him, latched right on to the nude gardening. The breeze didn't help, either, because it swirled her dress around again, this time lifting it up enough for him to get a glimpse of her thigh.

Her smile widened. "No loud parties, weddings in the pasture and I'll keep nude gardening to a minimum." She stuck out her hand. "Want to shake on that?"

Matt was sure he was frowning, but it had nothing to do with the truce she obviously wanted. It was because he was trying to figure out how the hell he was going to look out the kitchen window and not get a too-clear image of Emory naked except for gardening gloves.

He shook his head, but because the stupid part of him was still playing into this, his gaze locked on her mouth. That mouth he suddenly wanted to taste.

"The last time I kissed you, your brothers saw it and beat me up. Repeatedly," he grumbled.

No way had he intended to say that aloud. It'd just popped out. Of course, no way had he wanted to have the urge to kiss Emory, either.

"It's not a good idea for us to be living so close to each other," Matt managed to add.

"Don't worry," she said, her voice a sexy siren's purr. "You'll never even notice I'm here." With a smile that was the perfect complement to that purr, she fluttered her fingers in a little wave, turned and walked toward the cottage.

Matt just stood there, knowing that what she'd said was a Texas-sized lie. Oh, yeah, he would notice all right.

Don't miss
Summer at Stallion Ridge
by Delores Fossen, available April 2022 wherever
HQN books and ebooks are sold.

HQNBooks.com

PHDFEXP0322

Five years of memories didn't compare an ounce to the man
they'd been made about. Not when he seemingly materialized
out of midair, wrapped in a uniform that fit nicely, topped
with a cowboy hat his daddy had given him and carrying
some emotions behind clear blue eyes.

Eyes that, once they found Mel during her attempt to flee
the hospital, never strayed.

Not that she'd expected anything but full attention when
Sterling Costner found out she was back in town.

Though, silly ol' Mel had been hoping that she'd have more
time before she had this face-to-face.

Because, as much as she was hoping no one else would
catch wind of her arrival, she knew the gossip mill around
town was probably already aflame.

"I'm glad this wasn't destroyed," Mel said lamely once
she slid into the passenger seat, picking up her suitcase in the
process. She placed it on her lap.

She remembered leaving her apartment with it, but not
what she'd packed inside. At least now she could change out
of her hospital gown.

Sterling slid into his truck like a knife through butter.

The man could make anything look good.

"I didn't see your car, but Deputy Rossi said it looked like someone hit your back end," he said once the door was shut. "Whoever hit you probably got spooked and took off. We're looking for them, though, so don't worry."

Mel's stomach moved a little at that last part.

"Don't worry" in Sterling's voice used to be the soundtrack to her life. A comforting repetition that felt like it could fix everything.

She played with the zipper on her suitcase.

"I guess I'll deal with the technical stuff tomorrow. Not sure what my insurance is going to say about the whole situation. I suppose it depends on how many cases of amnesia they get."

Sterling shrugged. He was such a big man that even the most subtle movements drew attention.

"I'm sure you'll do fine with them," he said.

She decided talking about her past was as bad as talking about theirs, so she looked out the window and tried to pretend for a moment that nothing had changed.

That she hadn't married Rider Partridge.

That she hadn't waited so long to divorce him.

That she hadn't fallen in love with Sterling.

That she hadn't—

Mel sat up straighter.

She glanced at Sterling and found him already looking at her.

She smiled.

It wasn't returned.